The Princelings of the East

Book 1 of the series of the same name

Jemima Pett

Cover illustration by Danielle English kanizo.co.uk
Chapter illustrations by the author.

Other books in this series
The Princelings and the Pirates
The Princelings and the Lost City
The Traveler in Black and White
The Talent Seekers
Bravo Victor

Princelings Publications
The Princelings of the East
© J M Pett 2011-15
Blurb Edition 2.1

This book is dedicated to
Dawn Cavalieri

Contents

Principal Characters

At Castle Marsh:

Princeling Fred – A natural philosopher by inclination, and an adventurer at heart

Princeling George - Fred's twin brother, an engineer with lofty ideas

King Cole XIV – a king with a lot on his mind

Prince Vladimir (Uncle Vlad) – Cole's natural successor and second in command

At the Inn of the Seventh Happiness:

Victor – a harried barkeeper who doesn't waste words except on royalty; there's more to him than meets the eye

Gandy – his ancient assistant

Argon – an absentee landlord, not by choice, and Victor's father

Hugo – a travelling business person selling Wozna Cola, who is definitely not what he seems

At Castle Buckmore:

Prince Lupin – a playboy at heart, but a king in truth

Lady Nimrod – the wisdom behind the throne

Baden – the castle's steward

At Castle Hattan:
   Lord Mariusz – King of his castle, and adopter
   of pseudonyms
   Professor Saku – mad inventor, or just a genius
   Raisin – one of many employees, but who takes
   his job more seriously than most

At Castle Vexstein:
   Lord Smallweed – a nasty piece of work, second
   in line to the throne, who's looking forward to
   absolute power
   Baron (Lord) Darcy – Smallweed's elder
   brother, who enjoys leaving the hard work to
   him
   Pogo – an unspecified relation, possibly in line
   for the throne some day, making the most of his
   opportunities

Chapter 1: The Castle in the Marsh

In which we meet the young Princelings and a good feast is ruined

George was suspended in mid-air, his legs dangling from the ceiling of one room while his arms scrabbled furiously for a hold on the floor of the room above. He was trying very hard to do it silently, but it was a bit difficult.

He had jumped up through the trap door in the ceiling as usual, then realised his brother Fred was gazing out of the open window. So he had stopped in mid-jump, but now gravity was taking over. They were in this top-most tiny room in the turret of the castle, their ancestral home. If Fred was gazing out of the window across the miles of marsh that surrounded them, that meant he was Thinking.

Fred was apt to be grumpy if disturbed in the middle of a Think. So George had a dilemma: to hold on tight and keep quiet, or drop back again and risk making a noise landing on the accumulated junk in the room below him.

Fred was often found gazing out of the window, any window would do, but this one was his favourite. He was also much given to Thinking, and at present he was thinking about the wind in the reeds. *If the wind is blowing in my face,* he thought, *why is it blowing the reeds in different directions around the castle?* If anyone asked his occupation, Fred described himself as a Natural Philosopher, a person who thinks about the whys and wherefores of nature, trying to understand how the world works. *I need to explore the nature of the wind. If only I can persuade George to devise some way of mapping what the wind is doing as it blows across the marsh and into the castle. Yes,* he thought, *that is the way forward,* and he sighed.

An answering sigh met his and George clambered the rest of the way into the room. He looked rather relieved that he had found a way to attract Fred's attention without interrupting him mid-Think.

"We might be in trouble, Fred," he said. "My latest engine stopped working. The trouble is everything in the castle stopped working at the same time. Uncle Vlad is not happy."

"Does he blame you?" Fred asked, with a frown, as he was sure it couldn't be George's engineering experiments causing the problem. This Energy

Drain had been happening every now and then for years now, and he had Thought about it a few times. There was no relationship with any of George's experiments. Nor with Young Boris's either, although Young Boris had been banished for causing it over three years ago. He was one of their many cousins, all grandchildren of the present King, but there were hardly any left in the castle now.

"I don't think so," replied George, "but Ludo keeps telling him he ought to root out the troublemakers before the King starts blaming him for the problem."

"Ludo can't have anything to do with it. He's always off sailing that boat of his down at the Big Water."

"No, of course not. He meant the King blaming Uncle Vlad."

"Uncle Vlad is the King's right-hand man. He does all the work round here. I'm sure he wouldn't blame Uncle Vlad," said Fred, but he paused and thought about it all the same.

He considered the way his cousins had left the castle; one by one they had set out for the great unknown. Sometimes they were escorted off the premises by the king's henchman, sometimes they had slipped out in the middle of the night. He and George had been out of the castle of course; they had travelled the marsh extensively and knew all the little side tracks and alleyways well. They even knew which ones were wet at different times of day; he and George had worked out a few years ago that while the wetness didn't coincide with the high tides at Summernot, on the coast, they did follow a similar pattern. George had engineered an ingenious measuring and timing device for this project, with a ball that floated up in a column of the rising water, and marked the height on a circular card that revolved with the clock as it did so. George was clever at that sort of thing. Fred wanted to get him to engineer something to measure the wind direction. He wondered how he could ask him. He looked out of the window for inspiration, and George joined him leaning on the windowsill.

"What do you make of the wind, brother?" Fred asked.

"Well, I *was* making an engine to use the wind to make some more energy for the castle," George complained. "But it's a bit difficult to test it when I have to do it inside, with no wind, and the energy runs out any time I try to use it to make some wind."

"Why don't you do it outside?"

George sighed, and didn't reply.

Fred looked sideways at him. "What's wrong, brother?"

"I'm getting worried about drawing attention to ourselves. I'm sure this engine would be really useful for the castle, but with the disappearances and so on, I just think we should keep ourselves hidden from view."

"Do you mean we should stay clear of all the castle gatherings as well?"

"Yes, I do. I mean, most people don't know us and, apart from the food, the gatherings are a waste of time. I could be working on one of my projects and you could be Thinking. What I don't want is for people to interfere with my engines or take them over to make them *useful* for some other purpose."

Fred nodded. That had happened a couple of times when George had been making something with a Grand Plan in mind. Bits had been taken away by other people for makeshift solutions. Take the water-lifter that George had designed as an integral part of an irrigation system for the castle gardens. It had been commandeered and was now used at the castle entrance to move water from one side of the gate into buckets on the other. It was a complete waste of time. Then someone had wanted to put their names onto the rota to move the buckets! If they had used George's project as he'd designed it there wouldn't be any need to move buckets. Fred wondered whether this was how it had happened with the other princelings before them. Either they left of their own accord when they didn't fit in to the community, or they kicked up a fuss and were kicked out.

"We keep ourselves pretty well hidden these days, though," he mused, his thoughts going full circle to the problem of being seen about the castle.

"It's very comfortable living in the castle but it is getting far more difficult to keep hidden. And I can't make my engines and test them without going outside. People see me, and they push into my little cellar and want to use it for other things," George was in complaining mode now.

"Yes," Fred said, to stop George getting the Grumps. "The longer King Cole reigns, the more strangers seem to live here. Someone asked me who I was the other day."

"What did you say?" George smiled.

"I looked very snooty and said 'Don't you know?' and walked off quickly," Fred replied. "Then I got behind the tapestry in the next corridor very fast and scampered up here, I think, making sure no-one was following."

Fred and George knew how to take care of themselves: they had plenty of hidey-holes, had a fair knowledge of the labyrinthine secret passages of the castle, and best of all, were extremely quick at thinking of good answers to difficult questions.

"So you think we should avoid the next gathering completely?" he continued.

"Yes, we should," said George. Then he hesitated. "Although..."

"...it's the King's birthday gathering," completed Fred and it was his turn to sigh.

The King's birthday was the highlight of the castle's social calendar. Apart from the best feast, the best entertainment, and the best of the castle's wine cellar, it was also where the king gave out favours to anyone that presented themselves in the proper form, and where favours were sometimes bestowed on persons who had no idea they were going to receive them. Fred and George wanted no favours, but it was usually fun to watch people receive them. Especially as some favours were appropriate gifts to the receiver, and ones they might not actually like. Like the new anvil that was given to the blacksmith one year, that took away his excuse for not getting things done in time. The blacksmith was a lazy person, and Fred chuckled to himself at the memory of his face.

"Could we watch from the gallery?" asked Fred, hoping they could at least see some of the persons he and George least liked getting something they didn't want.

"The musicians will be in the gallery," George responded, "and we wouldn't be able to get to the food, so we'd be frustrated."

"And Uncle Vlad would probably spot us," Fred agreed gloomily. "When is it, anyway?"

"Two days time."

***

The music was good, the Great Hall was crowded, and their grandfather, King Cole XIV, was circulating among his subjects followed by a retinue of persons carrying packages of varying shapes and sizes. Fred and George had solved their problem by hiding in a sizeable alcove that was covered by a tapestry. The alcove was usually solely occupied by a marble statue of King Rudolph II. The tapestry was usually found hanging in the second corridor to the west of the upper circle of the main castle. It had a fair size patch that was extremely threadbare where countless bottoms had rubbed against it as they turned a tight corner to go down to the dining hall three or more times a day. Fred had spotted the patch and George had confirmed it was not only the right height for them but it was also as easy to see through as a fine veil. Moving it the night before had been an interesting task, but they had made it without being seen by anyone that mattered. They had to share the space with King Rudolph, but they had slipped into the kitchens before the event started and stocked up with a selection of the cold foods already prepared. The smell of the hot food in the ovens had been mouth-watering, and they regretted missing the main feast. They'd made up for it by bringing back loaded plates. Garnishes and bits of sandwiches and half-eaten vegetable sticks were all that remained on them. Some of the empty ones were stacked on top of King Rudolph's crown and the rest cradled pretty safely between the top of his shield and his right arm. They were still hoping to sneak out to sample the cooked food though. It seemed to them to be very late arriving.

They watched as the King did the rounds. Prince Vladimir, the Princelings' uncle and the King's deputy, looked straight at them, or rather the tapestry, a couple of times.

"I don't like the looks Vlad keeps giving us," Fred whispered to George.

"He can't see us," said George. "Stop feeling guilty!"

"He knows this shouldn't be here."

"So what's he going to do about it right now?"

What Prince Vladimir was going to do was walk right over to them. He stood there eyeing the tapestry, lips pursed. He reached out to the side of

8

the tapestry. Fred and George held their breath, looking at each other with wide eyes.

"Your highness," said a servant, scurrying up behind the prince and whispering urgently in his ear so loudly that Vlad flinched and Fred and George could hear him. "We have a problem in the kitchen."

Vlad turned. "What?" he said sternly.

"The ovens, they stopped working some time ago, we don't know when. The cook..."

"Why didn't you notice?" Vlad barked.

"Well, they were all working flat out, things were cooking, smelling of cooking, sizzling, and then they stopped sizzling, but the noise around was so loud we didn't notice," stammered the servant.

"Well, serve what you can; it should have been served half an hour ago!"

"That's the problem, sire," said the servant. "The cook is in tears, it's all ruined!"

"Surely something can be served?"

"Some accompanying sauces, sire, but the pies and pastries ruined, the soufflé sunk, the vegetables are rock hard and the puddings a glutinous mess."

Just then the music stopped.

"Wait here! No, get the cook to put the sweetmeats out."

They both hurried away, Vlad to the minstrels gallery where he could be heard remonstrating with the bandleader and the servant, presumably, to the kitchen.

George looked at Fred wide-eyed.

"The Energy Drain again! Oh, my - at such a time."

Fred nodded. "Everything on full blast, and the special lighting and everything. Just too much load, I suppose."

"The castle's power plant should have no problem coping with this load. Something is draining the energy, Fred. And it certainly isn't us!"

Chapter 2: Consequences

window on the Marsh

In which George loses his Engine, the castle reveals a Secret, and Fred has an Idea

For the next two days, the Princelings kept well hidden but used every secret passage they knew to listen to everything that was going on in the castle. Recriminations were everywhere. Everyone was accusing everyone else of ruining the King's birthday gathering. Their best source of information was from their favourite hidey-hole, a little space behind the chimney in their uncle's apartment. They could hear what he said to anyone when he was there. They couldn't hear his thoughts though.

"I don't like it, Fred, it seems that anything that uses energy is being examined and destroyed unless it's vital. I'd better go and hide my wind engine. But where should I put it?"

"We could move it up to the tower. No-one knows how to get into it."

"How on earth will we get the machine in there though?"

Fred paused, imagining the wind engine, the entrance to the tower, and the difficulty of lifting it through the gap.

"Let's get it there now, and then take it through piece by piece if necessary."

They slipped out of the little room and along the corridor, then into the room beyond the entrance to Uncle Vlad's apartments. They closed the door quietly behind them, went to the third wooden panel and leaned against it. The panel slid aside, the brothers slid through and were off down some narrow stairs with the panel shutting with a gentle hiss behind them. They emerged in the basement, just along from the kitchen, and crept along to the door down to the cellars. After a couple of twists and turns, George turned into the alcove where he did his work. He stopped dead with an anguished cry, which he stifled immediately.

Fred looked over his shoulder. The wind machine lay in pieces on the floor in front of them, wooden struts broken, cloth sails ripped, cogs torn from their spindles, the casing smashed in. He put his hand on George's shoulder.

"Can you rescue anything from this?"

George nodded, tears welling in his eyes. He always kept everything, never knowing when he might just need a piece of wood such a length, or a cog sized just so. They gathered it all together, putting it in a bag that had somehow escaped the wreckers' attention, and hauled it up with them, back up stairs, along corridors, and up to their favourite tower. George stood looking out of the window and Fred busied himself with the making of a soothing drink. He couldn't understand why anyone would smash George's work up; everything George did was for the benefit of the castle. Only an amazingly ignorant person would imagine otherwise. He would probably have to give up any hope of getting George to help him with mapping the wind. He did so much want to understand why it blew the reeds this way and that around the castle.

At length George turned back from the view and came to sit beside Fred.

"Well, we did say we'd bring it through piece by piece if necessary," he said with a weak grin and a sniff. "They are just smaller pieces than I'd anticipated."

Fred smiled at him and gave him a hug. "That's the spirit, George, chin up and all that. I'll help."

That brought a slightly firmer smile to George's lips. Fred's help when building things was not usually of great value, but he didn't want to hurt his feelings so he said nothing.

"The only trouble with staying up here out of sight," said Fred, "is that we might miss something important."

"I got the impression that Vlad is building up to some sort of announcement," George said.

"Yes, although I don't understand what as he really doesn't know what's causing it."

"Have you had any ideas about it?"

"No, although I don't think it's anything we're doing in the castle; there's no reason for it."

"I wonder if it's happening everywhere then, and what other people do about it?"

George and Fred both sat and thought on that. 'Other people', people from other castles, did not usually figure much in their thoughts.

"When did we last see a messenger here?" Fred asked.

"Last winter there was the person who came from Castle Wash. He was a good chap."

They grinned as they remembered an entertaining evening they had with the messenger that had brought greetings from the nearest castle to their own king. The brothers had waylaid him on his departure. They had persuaded him to stay the night after a few ales, a lot of gossip, and by the thought of a nice bed in front of a warm fire rather than a dark journey in the freezing marshes.

"He didn't tell us much about the outside world though." Fred sighed. "There was that stranger who came by coach a year or two ago, the one we never actually saw, only spoke to Vlad and the King."

"The lady, you mean?"

"Well, you thought she was a lady."

"I bet she was."

"Well, given we don't even know whether she was a lady, let alone where she (if he was a she) came from, or what she spoke to uncle and grandfather about all alone, no servants or anything, I don't know that we can count her as a messenger."

Fred stood up. "I'm going back downstairs. It's good to look at the marshes and Think, but we're not getting anywhere. I want to know what's going on, and I won't find out sitting here. And you aren't in the mood to build more engines. Let's go back down and do some more listening."

***

"Uncle Vladimir has ordered everyone to attend in the Great Hall at sunset for an announcement," Fred said, with a grimace. "So I think we'd better slide in at the back to hear what's going on."

George nodded. They had returned to the cubbyhole behind Vlad's apartments. After a few minutes of fidgeting, Fred said he was going out to find out what was going on. George was feeling miserable, so he stayed there. He'd spent a little time scribbling notes, setting down what he'd learned from the ruined wind engine, and then found himself sketching something that might help Fred map the wind around the castle. As grief over one machine turned to excitement over a new project, George bucked up. Fred had returned from his investigations just in time to stop him building something new on the spot.

George explained to Fred his sketches for a wind-mapping machine, and Fred spent a little time getting excited and imagining all sorts of grand designs that could follow on, but this was obviously not going to be work to start one late afternoon. As sunset drew near, the boys made their way down to the Great Hall. They sidled into the Great Hall just as Vlad walked up to the front and onto a low raised platform. He turned to face them and cleared his throat.

"Thank you all for coming," he said politely. "You are all aware that the King has been losing Energy recently. The shambles of the Birthday Gathering was shameful and everyone who contributed to our disgrace has been exiled. We have decided that the Energy Drain has to stop and therefore everyone here must conserve Energy. Anyone found using Energy without a permit will be severely dealt with." A buzz went round the Hall as various people asked their neighbours what the nature of 'severely dealt with' might mean. Vladimir paused and looked at them sternly, and the noise subsided.

"You are also to be watchful. Energy Eaters have been seen in the neighbourhood! Drive them out! Kill them on sight! Do not rest until we have driven them from our midst! That is all." And he strode from the platform and disappeared through a narrow doorway.

Fred and George made an equally quick exit. They made a beeline for their warm and comfortable cubbyhole. They rested on some tapestry cushions, acquired after the disastrous birthday gathering, and discussed the meaning of the pronouncement.

"Energy eaters - that's daft," said Fred. "Those little

wormy things are around again, they always are at
this time of year."

"Exactly so," said George, "and I am sure they make
the little lights they carry from the food they eat.
They hardly ever come in the castle anyway."

"Is it a bluff, do you think? Uncle Vlad can't
possible think the wormy things are really Energy
eaters, can he?"

"I don't think so, but grandfather might. He is rather
superstitious."

"There must be other castles affected by this Energy
Drain," mused Fred. "We don't even know how
many castles there are in this land." They had heard
of one or two, but they hadn't even travelled to
Castle Wash.

"I don't know," replied George. "We need to get
messages to other castles ourselves, to gather
information from them. If only we knew some
people there whom we could trust."

"What we need," said Fred "is a secret passage that
connects with the other castles - a tube network."
There was a sudden groaning noise and a dreadful
shaking of the floor. A large hole appeared in the
corner of the room. George went over to look at it.

"It appears to be a tunnel of some sort," he said.
"There are stairs leading down into it coming out of
the rock."

"It's never been there before...," said Fred, with a
stunned look on his face.

"I think you asked for it, and the castle provided you
with one," George replied in a matter-of-fact tone.

"Have you ever specifically said that you needed something before and it turned up?"

"Well," said Fred slowly," I think I have said I need a drink of water before now ... and there was usually a jug or a tap round the next corner. But I don't often say I need something - because I don't, not often, anyway."

George nodded. They tended to make do with what they had, and use their wits for most other things. And Fred wouldn't say he needed something, he would say "I could do with" something that could achieve his desire, not "I need it".

"Well," George said, "Are we going to see whether this tunnel connects with other castles, or shall we just sit and look at it?"

Fred sat staring at the tunnel, lost in thought. George waited. This might take a while. He could hear soft sounds of crackling flames in the fire on the other side of the wall, and in the distance the occasional pitter-patter of footsteps echoing down the corridors. He wondered what would happen if they ventured out of this castle into the tunnels. When he had been out in the marshes, he'd never gone a long way from home; the castle was always visible in the distance, light glinting on its spires. He'd never been out overnight, either. He identified a strange feeling inside him. They might be on the edge of a Great Adventure, but he wasn't sure he wouldn't rather be safely tucked up in bed.

Fred stirred. "We need to go and investigate this Great Energy Drain," he said. "We must find out whether it is a widespread phenomenon, and whether the causes are known."

George nodded; this was elementary procedure for an investigation. "And then?" he asked.

"And then," answered Fred, "we shall come up with some ideas for how to solve it."

"Good idea!" said George, knowing that you can never know exactly how you are going to do something until you have made the preliminary investigation and tested out a few theories. But the aim was set, and all they had to do now was decide... to go or not to go?

So they looked at each other, then jumped down the hole onto the steps and down into the tunnel, not knowing where it would all end.

Chapter 3: The Tunnel Network

The Tunnel

In which Fred meets a Mysterious Stranger and George finds a Sky Courtyard

The drip drip drip from the ceiling of the tunnel and the patter patter patter of their feet on the tunnel floor seemed to have been going on for hours. Or days. *Or even weeks*, thought George. It was still damp underfoot, and it still smelled of, well, marsh - which was not surprising since the castle was surrounded by it. But surely they should have passed beyond the marsh by now? Was the tunnel actually leading them in a huge circle?
"I could really do with a rest," he called softly forward to Fred, who was leading the way as usual.
"I was hoping to find somewhere dry," was the response.

George said nothing, just put his head down and carried on doggedly. 'Dry' would be nice too.

He was thinking about nice things like dry, warm and food when he bumped into Fred's behind, mainly because it was suddenly stationary. Fred grumbled softly but didn't otherwise complain.

"The tunnel makes a sharp turn ahead," he explained. "I just thought we ought to be cautious."

George made a grunt of agreement and they crept forward to the bend.

They peered round the corner to see a faint glimmer of light. As they crept forward the tunnel bent once again to make a zigzag. In the distance, some light cut into the tunnel at an angle.

"Well, something looks interesting up there," said Fred.

"More importantly," said George, "it is nice and dry under our feet, and we could just have a short rest and plan our next move." He sat down with a good stretch of his limbs to make a nice resting position on the now dry sandy floor of the tunnel.

"Well, I think it's fairly obvious that we go and find where that light is coming from," said Fred, likewise finding a nice comfortable position to rest. He muttered quietly to himself as he pondered on the nature of the light.

"It doesn't look like daylight, but it's steady, so it isn't firelight. There's not much air movement in the tunnel so I don't think it's an opening onto the outside world. It's too bright to be artificial. We're just going to have to go and investigate." So saying, he got up and went along the tunnel to have a look. He had no idea that George had fallen fast asleep and heard nothing of his musings.

As Fred drew closer, the light seemed to take on a translucent quality. He was only about twenty steps from where it shone into the tunnel when something blocked the light; a shadow fell across the tunnel, a shadow of something huge. Fred stood stock-still, barely daring to breathe. He briefly considered turning round and running, but didn't want George to think he was a coward. Something large, black and pointed protruded into the tunnel from the place where the light had been. It was attached to a face with black beady eyes that followed the nose out then looked each way up and down the tunnel. On its second look in Fred's direction, it stopped and fixed its gaze on him.

"Urr, well, hi," it said.

Fred was relieved that it spoke, which was a good sign, but bemused by the strange way in which it spoke. He decided that it was a greeting of sorts and needed a response.

"Greetings and good health to you and your family." he replied formally.

"Mighty kind of you I'm sure."

The owner of the beady eyes stepped out into the tunnel, dressed in a very snazzy black and white suit, with a crest just like Fred's, but white. Fred had never seen such an outlandish get-up but decided he was travelling, and maybe there were lots of outlandish things in the outlands. He turned to make a comment to George and was stunned to find George was not there. *Oops, no back up, just when you really need it*, he thought. He turned back to the stranger.

"My name is Fred, and I've travelled from the Castle in the Marsh," he introduced himself, expecting the stranger to do the same.

"Are you now? Well, that is interesting. Have you been travelling long?" asked the stranger, but instead of waiting for an answer, he carried on talking as if to himself and replying to his own question. "Has he been travelling long, what does that mean? Well, I suppose it could be useful knowing whether to check that way out or whether to carry on as usual."

"Um, well, I'm going to one of the other castles to see if they have any problems like the Energy Drain," Fred offered, to see if that would get more information from the stranger.

"Yeah, well, there're lots of castles in that direction and I don't reckon I've ever seen a castle in that direction before," the stranger said, nodding first at the way Fred was going and then at the way they had come. "If you've got an Energy Drain down there, there's no reason for going that way."

"Which way are you planning to go?" asked Fred.

"Oh, my usual, I s'pose," said the stranger. "No point in changing for the sake of changing." He gave Fred a piercing look. "You gonna tag along with me till we get there?"

Fred swallowed. He was tempted, but suddenly realised that he might lose touch with George. They had never been apart before. Well, apart from when one was Thinking and the other was, well, whatever it was George did when Fred was Thinking.

The stranger moved off, and Fred found himself following. *Well,* he thought, *George is hardly going to do anything other than follow along this tunnel, is he?* And because the light had gone out from where the stranger had emerged, Fred never thought about the tunnel forking off to the left as he hurried to run alongside the stranger, and the main tunnel widened as if to allow two-way traffic.

* * *

George awoke, feeling cold. Usually when he and Fred were asleep they kept each other warm. His tummy lurched as he realised that Fred was no longer there, and probably had not been there for some time. *How long have I been asleep,* he thought, *and why did Fred go off?*

He fought down a sense of panic growing inside him and told himself to be sensible. Fred would not have gone far without him. The trouble is, which way had he gone? And, as George had turned around in his sleep, which way was which? The feeling of panic grew stronger, but his head took over and worked out that the way home would feel damp, and the way forward would hopefully be dry. "I wonder what became of that light?" he said out loud.

He dithered a few moments longer as the attraction of going home called. *But if Fred wasn't there, how attractive would it be? No, the only way was onward,* so he put his nose towards the dry side and headed off round the corner and along the tunnel where earlier the light had shone in.

Soon he came upon the place where the tunnel widened and he saw that it forked. *Oh, no,* he thought, *which way now?* Fred's lingering scent was overlain with the scent of another, so that it was almost masked completely. The other scent was in both tunnels. There was a very slight glow a little way along the left hand tunnel, as if a ring of faint glow-worms was crawling right around the sides, ceiling and floor of the tunnel.

"Fred must have gone to investigate this light," he muttered to himself. "This must be the one he chose." He strode forward confidently.

As he passed the glowing ring, it burst into light. It felt like it lifted George off his feet and whooshed him along a slide made of sparkling, swirling light. "Oo-er" he said, clenching his tummy to stop both panic and travel sickness. It was over in a matter of seconds, however, and George emerged from the end of a tunnel onto a grassy square bathed in sunshine. He stood there, blinking in the bright sunlight, wondering what had just happened.

"Stay where you are, you are completely surrounded!" ordered a voice behind him. George stayed stock-still. A small black and tan person came up beside him. "Sorry about that, but you are," he said. "Welcome to the castle of Hattan - you are completely surrounded, because you're in our sky courtyard!" and the little one laughed, watching George's discomfiture.

"Greetings and good health to you and your family," he said politely. "My name is George. Would you mind telling me slightly more about where I am?"

"Hi, George, my name is Raisin. Come over here and look at the view!"

George accompanied his new, apparently young friend across to one side of the courtyard and looked out through great stone arches, over low walls planted up with strawberries, to the view beyond. Like his own home, Castle Hattan was on an island, but this island was full of towers festooned with greenery, mostly square towers, some with pointed tops, some with nice pyramids, and some with cones. They reached far down into the depths of the island, where they disappeared into a murky oneness that seemed to hum with people and machines. Beyond the towers was water, long strings of it that came together in a bay to the south where the sun reflected on it.

George recognised nothing. *It all seems rather futuristic,* he thought.

"Isn't it great?" asked Raisin. George nodded, astounded. "You can look at it any time you're here," continued Raisin, "But now I think I'd better take you to the Boss."

George followed Raisin to the corner of the courtyard where they went through an arch and down a few steps to the entrance of a comfortable apartment.

Raisin stopped at the door and coughed. "Come in" came a voice from inside. Raisin stepped aside and waved George through. "This is George, Uncle Mariusz," he said, and he turned and left.
George went forward and saw a large person, in a black and white coat, examining him with his black beady eyes.
"Urr, well, hi, George." he said. "I've kinda been expecting you."

Chapter 4: At the Inn of the Seventh Happiness

Seventh Happiness

In which Fred learns more about the Energy Drain and we meet a Prince with a Purpose

Fred's feet were getting sore. It was hard work running alongside the stranger. He didn't seem to be hurrying, yet he moved quickly for a big guy. At first Fred had chatted to the stranger freely, talking about life at the Castle, about George's experiments and engineering feats, about the cousins that had disappeared and about Uncle Vlad. Then he had got tireder and talked less, and they probably had not spoken for a couple of hours now. He wished he had taken George's advice and had a good rest. He felt guilty and worried at the same time; what would happen to George if he didn't catch them up? He would hardly be likely to at the pace they were going. Fred had been looking for somewhere to rest for ages, but there didn't seem to be anywhere, just miles and miles of unending smooth earth tunnel wall. He was summoning up the strength to suggest they stopped for a break just where they were, when they rounded a bend and he saw light ahead, not cold light like before, but warm, welcoming light, with a hum of voices.

They slowed to a stroll and came out of the tunnel into what appeared to be a market square, with other tunnels leading off at angles. It was night, but there were lanterns strung around the place and across from the tunnels to a building at the centre. Its windows and doors were wide open, and quite clearly was an inn. Fred's spirits brightened tremendously.

"Let's stop here and rest a while," said the stranger. Fred agreed heartily and they threaded their way through other travellers who were seated at tables, on benches and just on the floor, and arrived at the bar. A young person, with a cute face, greyish coloured hood covering hair that went everywhere at once, and wearing a smart white jacket was springing about from customer to customer. He waved cheerily at them and finished serving the traveller he was with.

"My goodness, Hugo!" he said, "We haven't seen you for ages! Where have you been?"

"Here and there," replied Hugo, for now the stranger had a name, "wherever business took me. How is your father?"

A shadow crossed the barkeeper's face. "He disappeared back in the early spring. Said he was going to look for more Energy. We haven't seen him since. What will you two have? Will you want to stay for the night? We have only one spare room. Sorry!"

Hugo accepted the spare room on their behalf and asked for a Wozna. He looked at Fred, who wondered what a Wozna was and asked for a strawberry juice to be safe. Hugo looked at him curiously, but just ordered the strawberry juice. When it arrived, he held it up to the light as if examining it for purity before passing it over.

"Your good health," said Hugo.

"And to your family," responded Fred and they breathed deep as they savoured their first drink for quite a while. Fred's tummy promptly rumbled and Hugo ordered a double portion of Melange du Jardin from the menu, which sounded good to Fred, as long as it was tasty and edible. They took a second round of drinks to a table in one corner where it was a little less boisterous: some of the travellers had started a game of Shove H'penny and there was quite a lot of Shoving going on.

They relaxed and looked around at the other customers. An enormous platter of fresh vegetables that the barkeeper brought over to them diverted their attention.

"Thanks, Victor," said Hugo. "That's real good. When you've got time, come and join us."

"Yes of course," he replied and scuttled off to serve more customers.

Fred and Hugo tucked in to the meal. It was delicious - plain, but revitalising, especially after a busy day travelling. In fact, Fred realised with a jolt, he must have been travelling for a whole day without really stopping. No wonder he felt tired and footsore.

"Where do you come from, Hugo?" he asked after they had demolished at least three-quarters of their meal, hoping that by asking again at a more mellow moment he might actually get some information.

"Well, my name's not really Hugo," he replied. "But they call me that in these parts and it will do."

"Why Hugo?"

"Because by your standards I'm huge, and I come and I go, I think," and he laughed.

Fred wondered whether he had invented that name himself to suit his personality, but he decided it fitted, and he was unlikely to get further with it, so he changed the subject.

"Why would Victor's father go to look for more Energy and not come back?" he asked.

"I don't know, and I mean to draw out Victor on that subject before I make any further plans. Oh, there's Lupes - do you mind waiting here while I do a little business with him? Finish the food, order more if you want, and have more to drink - it's on expenses."

He got up and whilst he appeared to amble over to someone sitting in the opposite corner, he arrived quickly at his side. The object of his attention was surrounded by what appeared to be admirers although it also had the cosy feel that might have been princelings round an uncle. Fred was unable to see him clearly but he appeared to have fallen in some soot as he had a smut on his nose. Fred also didn't understand what Hugo meant by expenses, but the order to help himself was clear. He went over to the bar and asked Victor for another strawberry juice and a melon chaser.

Victor waved him back to his seat. "I'll bring it when ready, if you don't mind. Awful busy. It'll quieten down soon. Only overnighters stay past midnight."

Midnight! Fred was right then. He and George had left the Castle in the Marsh a little while after sunset, but could never have travelled this far in less than five hours. He got to Thinking about time, and how it could fly or drag. He got himself so lost in his Thought he was very nearly grumpy when Victor interrupted him with the food and drink, but remembered both his manners and his thirst just in time.

"Where's Hugo gone? Oh, he's over with Prince Lupin. I wanted to catch up with him. I haven't seen you before. Are you Hugo's new apprentice?" Victor asked, settling down beside him with a drink he had brought for himself.

"Um, no," said Fred, working out that only the last comment needed an answer. "I was travelling with my brother George and we met Hugo when he came into the tunnel we were in."

"Brother George? I haven't served him yet." Victor looked around worried, like someone failing in his duty.

"No, we got separated." Fred reassured him. "If he

turns up here after we've gone, will you tell him which way to go?" he asked anxiously.

"George will get my best attention," Victor assured him, which made Fred feel only slightly less guilty for abandoning him.

"And where are you from?" asked Victor.

"The Castle in the Marsh," replied Fred, wondering how long it would be before he got back there.

"Hmm, heard people claim their birthplace," said Victor. "Not met someone claiming to come straight from there."

"I don't think we're renowned as travellers," Fred smiled, "but lots of my cousins have gone travelling one way or another."

"Your brother George, he looks like you? Will I recognise him?"

"He's very alike, but slightly redder hair and he hasn't got a crest," explained Fred. "We're non-identical twins, but people often mix us up even with the different hairstyles. This is good strawberry juice," he added, hoping to turn the questioning round the other way.

"Thank you. We still get call for the traditional drinks. Most people drink Wozna or Vex these days."

"I've not heard of either of them."

"Castle Marsh must be off the network. You'd have had the trade otherwise. They're all the rage. Hugo is involved. Brought us Wozna years ago. Only drinks Wozna that one." Victor supped his drink, which was in a bottle marked 'VEX' in green lettering.

"We're having trouble with an Energy Drain," Fred decided he might as well start researching straight away. "You said your father had gone looking for more Energy."

"Yes, Energy drains periodically. Always worst when we're low on stocks. Got the usual sources, sun, water, pedal power. We have this clever game in the backyard. The kids love it. Climb up the top of a tower and swing off. Does great things for our energy store. Can't keep up though. Oh - I'd better get back!" and he got up as Hugo came back to the table accompanied by the tall handsome prince, who either had been incredibly messy as his feet were also covered in soot or, more likely, thought Fred, was of a particularly noble line and this was his royal regalia.

"No, stay, Victor," said the Prince and Hugo more or less in unison. "We want to hear more about your father," added the Prince.

"Prince Lupin, may I present Princeling Fred of Castle in the Marsh," said Hugo, as Fred bowed deeply and formally, with his Castle's special sign. "Fred, you are in the presence of Prince Lupin of Buckmore."

Fred stayed in position.

"OK, Fred, rise, I'm not that formal outside the castles themselves," said the Prince, seating himself comfortably by the table with his feet up. Fred grinned and relaxed. This was the sort of prince he liked. "Settle yourself back again. Victor, tell me more about your father - I hear he's gone wandering."

"Not wandering, begging your pardon, Prince," said Victor in a suitably modest tone and much more formally, "He was anxious about the drain on our Energy. He said he was going to find more."

"Which way did he go and when?" asked the Prince.

"Three moons ago, he set off after closure. Along the Corey-Vexstein line."

"Probably thought to check out what happened at the first castle to be affected," said Hugo to the Prince.

"Excuse me, Prince Lupin," said Fred, "but we also have a problem with the Energy Drain and I am tasked to find out more about it."

Lupin and Hugo both looked at Fred; Lupin with interest, assessing him in a positive light, and Hugo, well, Hugo's look was rather suspicious.

"Ok, young Fred," said the Prince, "I will give you a crash course in the Energy Drain, but first we must find out a little more about Victor's father, since Victor cannot come with us and keep the inn going."

Lupin started to ask Victor about his father, and the times when Energy seemed to be at its lowest. Fred found himself nodding in the warmth of the room, and although he caught words like "delivery" and "turnover" and "dynamo", they all seemed very distant, as did the word "Castle Buckmore" which seemed to be joined to the phrases "set off for" and "at first light". He came to with a start and tried to look as if he had been listening and thinking. Victor was just standing up, nodding in a different way, and thanking the Prince for his attention.

"Don't worry too much, young man," said the Prince to Victor, "you're doing a grand job here and your father will be proud of you. Keep up the good work; we would be in a sorry state if the Inn of the Seventh Happiness was to close."

"Now, Hugo," he said, turning to him as Victor scurried off, "if we are going to make progress on this we need to be careful, but we need to make haste since the situation is getting critical. I'll go and brief my lads, and get some sleep. I'll see you both in the morning in the breakfast room. Goodnight to you both." He nodded politely, Fred bowed again, and Lupin laughed gently as he strode off.

"Time to turn in," said Hugo. "The room's this way," and he led the way across the inn and down a staircase that corkscrewed into the corner.

"How far is it to Castle Buckmore?" asked Fred.

"We'll probably arrive before sundown if we get away at first light. I don't know what you did, but it made a good impression on the Prince. He's not usually too quick in taking up with other people - got too many of his own to look after."

They arrived at their room, a small cubbyhole, not much larger than the hidey-hole Fred and George had left at their own castle.

"You take that corner - sleep well, and get yourself up quickly when we're called - we need to be on our way pronto."

Fred shifted round Hugo to get to the corner and

settle down. He had plenty to Think about, but he really felt in need of sleep. He wondered what would happen at Castle Buckmore. He closed his eyes and stayed still for what seemed like five seconds before he wanted to scratch his leg. He opened his eyes again and started: someone was tickling his leg with a feather. Victor's face was looking out of a small hole in the floor at the foot of his bed. He put a finger to his mouth, warning him to be quiet, and beckoned Fred to follow him. Fred did so, even more quietly than a mouse, leaving Hugo gently snoring in the other corner. They went down a narrow tunnel then up some stairs and emerged into some well-lit, beautifully appointed rooms.

"Sorry, young Fred," said Prince Lupin. "I think you should leave now, with my friend and Steward here, the former Princeling Baden. He'll introduce you to someone who can explain when you get to Buckmore. You can sleep in the carriage."

Fred, not sure who could be trusted and who could not, decided to go with the flow. He got into a carriage for the first time in his life, and set off, with an unknown but amiable guy called Baden, into the dark of the night.

Chapter 5: Strawberry Juice

In which George discovers the world of Wozna and the real power of Strawberry Juice

George followed Raisin into the room where 'Uncle Mariusz' relaxed on a Japanese-influenced day bed. Souvenirs from all parts of the globe were artfully displayed: Javanese shadow puppets adorned one wall, corn dollies from George's own land were pinned over an empty fireplace. In one corner, there were some tribesmen's shields and spears, propped together to make a pleasing sculpture-like ensemble, and sheer fabric with an Indian design shimmering through it draped the windows.

In a cabinet running along the centre of the longest wall was a collection of bottles and cylindrical metal containers the like of which George had not seen before. They all bore, in different scripts and combinations, the words Wozna and Cola, and occasionally Diet.

"Come in and take a seat," said Mariusz, waving at some cushions on the floor, with what looked like a very valuable Turkish carpet underneath them. "You'll need some refreshment?"

"Oh, well that's very kind of you," said George, somewhat bemused at this welcome. "Please may I have a strawberry juice?" he added, politely.

"Urr, well, we don't drink strawberry juice around here, I'll show you why later." Mariusz said. "How about a Wozna?"

"A Wotta? Oh, I'm so sorry, I'm not familiar with it," he added hurriedly, remembering he was in a strange land with a stranger and needed to keep his wits about him a bit better. "Yes, I'd be pleased to try it. Is it a local speciality?"

Mariusz waved behind him and there was a scurrying noise; someone waiting to take the order had now left.

"Yeah, you could call it that," he said, getting up and moving towards the cabinet on the long wall. "It's the drink my granddaddy invented. We owe all of our success, the castle," waving around him, "all this, to Wozna."

Pointing out each of the bottles and containers, which he called cans, in the cabinet, he proceeded to give George the complete history of Wozna Cola. Founded by Zoltan Wozniak, his granddaddy (possibly with a couple of 'greats' thrown in), it became a staple in the great drought of '55 when all the fruit failed. The flavourings he invented managed to combine with the local spring water to give the locals a palatable and sustaining drink. Concerns over the increasing size of the average Hattanite led to the development of Diet Wozna, and trade had expanded over the last ten years thanks to Mariusz's efforts in finding new markets, thereby consolidating the family's position at the very top of Hattan society. George wasn't entirely sure what that meant, but that was what this large impressive person said.

Their drinks had arrived somewhere around the development of a new processing mechanism in the 2010s, and George had been momentarily distracted from the narrative as he sipped the cool, dark, flavoursome brew, slightly sweet and slightly tangy, with a hint of a fizz to it. Frankly, he'd rather have strawberry juice, he thought, nicer and it sounds less processed. Raspberry juice at a pinch. Or even water, although he kept his face looking interested, and he smiled and thanked his host when asked how he found it. "Oh, very refreshing, thank you!" Since he was thirsty, he continued to sip it.

Mariusz finished his narrative and George thanked him for the background. Something was worrying him about it.

"So you see, George," said Mariusz after a pause in which he took a long draught of his drink, "you've arrived at a most convenient moment for us, you couldn't have timed it better."

"Er, well, no, I mean, yes, I see," said George, not seeing at all. He looked into his drink, a little puzzled, and decided to wait for further information.

"We heard tell of your reputation as an engineer of uncommon skill, so we thought you might take a look see."

"Um, well."

George was torn between two questions. And the more he thought about them, the more he thought it better not to ask either: how did he know he was an engineer, or, take a 'look see' at what, which might show he hadn't been listening properly.

"OK, then. I'll be pleased to take a look." And he only thought, "at what?"

He finished his drink and Mariusz stood up and beckoned him over to the door that he had come in through.

"We'll go down to the lab and I'll introduce you to my scientific guru."

George followed him out into the afternoon sunshine across the courtyard where he'd arrived, and under another arch, leading down a number of flights of steps, where it got cooler as they went down. The slight humming noise that George thought he could hear when he arrived got louder. Eventually they stopped at a large door with a notice saying 'Authorized Personnel Only'. Mariusz opened the door and they went in.

They were standing in a huge room with a vaulted ceiling, and some high windows letting shafts of light onto the amazing construction in the middle of the floor. It had straight pipes and bottles and vats and steps and curly pipes and towers, and there were little wisps of steam escaping from even more pipes in various places. There was a rhythmic thudding noise and a few other occasional clunks, tinkles and gurgles as whatever it was did whatever it was doing. And a pleasant, low hum.

George stood and looked at it for a bit. It was certainly complicated, and he was willing to gamble that it was more complicated than it should be. It didn't look designed, it looked stuck together. But at present, he didn't know what it was supposed to do, let alone how it was supposed to do it.

"What do you think?" asked Mariusz.

"It's very impressive," replied George. "Who built it?"

"Oh, Saku built this one - he's probably round the back somewhere. Saku!" he called and a very hairy person with a wild look about his face popped his head round one of the towers from a gantry half way up it and waved.

"This is George, Saku. He's come to take a look at the machine." Mariusz turned to George. "I'll leave you with him, I'm sure you two will speak the same language - engineering and all. When you're ready, come back to my rooms," and with that he turned and left George with a strange machine, a mad scientist, and not the faintest idea what was going on.

* * *

42

It took Saku maybe an hour to give George a complete tour of the installation, explaining what everything did in minute detail. They started with the grain input hopper, filled from the silo at the back, and followed its journey through numerous processes of cooking, fermentation, straining and separation, before arriving at a point where it was mixed with the special ingredients. They then backtracked to the start of that process and went right up to the highest walkway to follow that through.

"This is where are special ingredients are fed in," Saku said. "I'm afraid I can't tell you what they are, I would, of course; it's a secret formula. I'm sure you understand."

"It's not important, as far as I'm concerned, unless it affects the processes involved," George replied.

After the two streams were mixed together there were some complicated processes involving modulisers and capacitors and distillators and compressors. George had a bit of trouble keeping up with all of the concepts as they were far in advance of anything he'd done himself, but he could see what they were supposed to do. He could also see that in a few places they were doing opposing things within a few yards of each other. He came to the end of the line, where it went into a bottling plant on the other side of a doorway.

"This is the secret section," Saku said. "Bottling is important technology of course, and we have revolutionised the way it's carried out. Our set-up is one that we franchise all over the world for anything that needs bottling. We earn a lot of money from it, apparently," and he shook his head in disbelief that something as mundane as bottling could be a moneymaking angle when what he was making was the real product.

Back in Saku's little study they relaxed in nice comfortable chairs, just like a sitting room at home. George couldn't rest though. He went over to the large desk and started mapping out the process, checking with Saku that he had understood it correctly. He had spotted a number of redundancies in the system as they went round, or thought he had. He started checking whether they still had a purpose now, even though they once did before various 'improvements' had been made. Apart from everything else, he had learned two very important facts: the source of the power supply, and that Saku was extremely pleasant and not a bit upset that a stranger had arrived to help him solve the problem. What he hadn't learned was precisely what the problem was. He wanted to understand the system, and what it was supposed to do, before he asked about that.

He completed his map and sat down, licking his lips. "Would you like a drink?" asked Saku, seeing his movement.

"Well, yes, please, but something a little more thirst quenching than Wozna, if you don't mind." He hoped that didn't sound rude, but he thought it best to be plain with Saku.

"Oh I know what you mean," he said, "I think we could afford to draw off a little of the strawberry juice."

"But I thought Mariusz said you don't drink strawberry juice here?"

"Well, we don't, but the power vat has to be regulated, doesn't it?" he said with a smug grin. He took out two glasses, one just a bit bigger than an eggcup, and the other about half as big again, and nipped outside to the largest silo. He turned a small tap near the base to fill the two glasses to the brim. He brought them back carefully.

"Your good health," he said.

"And that of your family," responded George, and he sipped the juice, which, instead of its usual pink colour, had taken on a beautiful golden glow, and was rather thicker than usual. It was amazing, even better than usual, and very thirst quenching in spite of the apparent lack of fluid in it. He pondered everything Saku had told him.

On first pointing out the silo of strawberry juice and explaining that it provided the power, Saku had laughed at George's bewilderment. He reminded him of the test everyone did at school when they first started understanding the nature of energy. They put a wire of one metal on one side of their tongue, and a wire of another metal on the other side, and felt the tingle as the power coursed across their tongue from one wire to the other, conducted by their saliva.

"It's the same with strawberry juice" he said, "only the power surge is astronomical and we have used it to power most of our needs ever since it was discovered."

That was why strawberries grew from so many balconies, as everyone had a small power plant for home use as well as the central grid powered by the community. It had revolutionised Hattan society, since it was no longer necessary to use small people to work the wheels that had generated power for centuries, and which had become more and more expensive since the abolition of slavery.

"Who actually discovered it?" George asked.

"It was invented in the east world," Saku replied vaguely, "but the technique swiftly spread worldwide. We got it very quickly here."

The burning question that George had in the background of his mind ever since Mariusz's talk rose to the surface. He was sure Mariusz had said something about a new processing mechanism in the 2010s. Yet he must have misheard, because it was only 2009 now. He was wondering how to establish the truth without sounding too foolish. Now he thought he knew how.

"So we've mapped out the process," he said, looking at his drawing once more. "What was the big change that Mariusz mentioned and when did that occur?"

"Oh well, that was the development of Diet Wozna in 2011," Saku replied, and George was sure he'd heard him right this time. "We'd been wondering how to pander to the new fad for slimming foods, and once strawberry power was available we could have all the extra energy that is needed to reduce the

Wozna from forty calories to one calorie per bottle (or can, really, because we only ever produce Diet in cans.)"

George's mind whirled. Apart from the stupidity of using all that extra energy to make a low energy drink (and where did all the energy go?), he was fairly sure that Mariusz said he had been exporting Diet Wozna for about ten years now. "So that makes it at least 2021," he muttered to himself.

"Sorry?" Saku said.

"I was just working out the time line," he said, keeping his voice steady and trying to stay relaxed. "You've been using strawberry power for over ten years, and it went in right at the start of the process," he covered himself, pointing at the process map.

"What was there before?"

"Oh, an ordinary grid inlet feed supporting a Carnot engine."

"And that went to the same pump?"

"Yes that's right."

George worked through the process again with Saku and sat back as he came to a conclusion.

"I think the pump is sized for the wrong power capacity," he said. "It's overworking. If it was sized to the higher energy input it could push a larger volume through more efficiently than these small volumes operating many more times in the same period."

It was fundamental to the entire operation. Fix that and the whole operation would be transformed, George thought, and then they could lose this step, and that machine, then straighten out that pipe run which would again enhance the efficiency... Was he really in 2021?

Saku was staring at the process map George had drawn. He stroked the hair behind his ear thoughtfully, then went out and looked at the pump, even though it was housed in a nice metal covering, so you couldn't actually see it. It was pumping away, with an occasional squeak and occasionally also a hiss.

Saku came back in, took up a blue pencil, made some changes to the pump, crossed out another machine, re-routed three pipe runs, and crossed out another process. "What do you think?" he asked George. "I agree," he said, with a smile. "Although you might find it useful to replace the thermal capacitor with a thermal moduliser as well, which would improve the overall efficiency of the heat co-generation."

"Brilliant!" said Saku. "I thought I was good, but you are exceptional, young George. All we need now is to work out whether the time tunnel is still draining our energy and if so, stop it!"

Chapter 6: The Energy Hunter

In which Fred meets the Energy Hunter and has to decide who to trust

Fred opened one eye and saw that a castle bathed in morning light was passing by the window as he was jolted gently along in the carriage. He opened the other and saw his companion doing a crossword puzzle in the opposite corner.

"Good morning!" said Baden. "When you're ready I'll unpack the breakfast basket that I brought with us in case of need."

Fred blinked and stretched. "Where are we? Is that Castle Buckmore? I thought that was where we were going?" he added with a momentary touch of panic as his confusion of last night returned.

"No, that is Castle Powell, my ancestral home,"

replied Baden, taking the lid off a basket he had pulled from under his seat. "The Buckmore-Powell tunnel comes out of the hill that leads down to Powell, but we go over the next set of hills and across the river on the regular road to get to Buckmore."

Relieved, Fred sat back and then leant forward to help Baden extract some fresh salad and dried fruit bars from the basket. Baden then took out a flask of water and two cups. Fred helped him munch his way through the supplies, enjoying the experience of a picnic with a passing view.

"If that's your ancestral home," commented Fred through mouthfuls, "why are you Steward at Buckmore?"

"It's a long story," Baden replied, "In short; I found it expedient to leave in order not to get drawn into family matters, like murder. Lupin needed a Steward, I got the job."

"Are you still a princeling though? Prince Lupin said 'former Princeling'."

"Well spotted. No, I gave up my claim, but with some people it's worthwhile them knowing you're from a noble line. I expect he wanted to make sure you took me seriously, as we don't know you yet."

They chatted about kings and castles, and Baden explained how the kings and lords met at the Kings' Council a number of times a year to keep the peace. He told stories about individuals without naming names as the road twisted and turned through the hills. After an hour or so, it emerged from gently wooded slopes down to a wide river. They rattled across a long wooden bridge and up a slight slope. "And there is Castle Buckmore," said Baden, leaning out of the window and pointing as they rounded a rock at the top of a small hill.

Not far away, on a low slab of rock with steep crags at one end, was a handsome residence. It appeared to have many trees inside courtyards protected by white walls with red-tiled roofs. Towers dotted the corners of various sections, and some looked like small bell-towers. Fred thought it looked charming, and although not particularly impressive, it had the air of understated grandeur that comes from a family that has no need to show off at all.

The carriage rattled through an arched gate at the lowest end of the rock, and along a dimly lit tunnel, where it had to do a strange manoeuvre of stopping as the tunnel turned, and then reversing a short way up the next stretch to another turn, where it could once again go forward up into the light.

"A simple but effective way of protecting the castle from invaders," explained Baden. "There is a shorter way in at the other end where we can give unwanted visitors a nasty taste of boiling oil as it is pretty much a vertical ascent!"

Fred was very glad he was not an unwanted visitor as they got out of the carriage in a sunlit plaza. It had a large stretch of grass and a few apple trees in the centre, bordered by a broad pavement of stone flags in front of market stalls and shops set into arches in the wall behind. Flags and drapery fluttering in the mild, sweet scented breeze. He breathed appreciatively as his feet regained solid ground and he felt the sun on his back for the first time in what seemed like weeks. Then he reminded himself not to relax too much as he was on a mission and hadn't decided who he could trust yet.

Baden saw to the organisation of the carriage and unloading of packages from the top of their compartment. Fred watched, wondering how someone learned to be a steward.

"Right, then, Fred," he said, walking across to the far corner of the plaza, "My orders were to take you to see Lady Nimrod, and she's expecting you."

Fred followed his companion past a fountain and up a shallow stone staircase at the side of the plaza. That led into a corridor that opened on to an adjacent courtyard. They went along that, through another archway into another similar corridor, then up more stairs, until Fred completely lost count of how many corridors and how many stairs they had gone up. Castle Buckmore was much more extensive than Castle Marsh, or was it mainly that he knew his way there? He couldn't decide. One thing he noticed as they walked the corridors was that there didn't seem to be a fixed ground point for the gardens in the centres of the courtyards. They never went down any steps, but one courtyard might be way below their walkway, and another only just the other side of the wall. That was the case as Baden halted at another arch. A right-angled turn would take them along the second side of a square at their own level, a square filled with scented flowers and herbs. There were rich drapes at the arches of the room that overlooked the garden.

"Wait here!" Baden said, and he went through the arch leaving Fred breathing the scent of the herbs, identifying in turn lavender, mint, thyme, oregano, pennyroyal, gillyflower, and some he didn't recognise but smelled really good.

A rustle at the door and a sweet, musky scent overlain with that of flowers he couldn't name brought him back to the immediate task, and a lady dressed in a white taffeta robe, again with the dark points that Prince Lupin had, came to the doorway and greeted him, holding out her hand.

"Welcome, young Fred, to Castle Buckmore. It has been years since there was contact between our families but I am most pleased to see you here, even though the circumstances are dark."

Fred bowed low, again holding his pose, making his secret sign and then kissing her outstretched hand.

"I thank you for your greeting, most gracious lady," he said, straightening up, and he followed her into the apartment beyond. It was one of the most beautifully decorated he had seen, with sheer drapes across the far windows letting in the light and billowing gently in the breeze. They took their seats on a shady terrace overlooking the garden and drinks arrived in plain but delicate china cups. This lady had style.

At first, Lady Nimrod asked Fred about recent events at Castle Marsh. He told her that King Cole was well, as was Prince Vladimir, but that some of his cousins had left to go into exile, but Prince Ludo was around, when he wasn't off sailing his boats. She showed considerable knowledge of his family history, including relatives he had never met, and discussed the ability of their land holding to supply food for all the inhabitants. She had obviously been there at some time although she was not familiar with the new wing that Uncle Vlad had built. Eventually he brought the conversation around to the Energy Drain, and told her about recent events. "So, although you were aware of a problem last year that has been continuing in an irritating manner," she summarised, "it was not until the disaster of the King's birthday party that you realised the problem was worse than you thought?" Fred nodded in agreement. "This pronouncement by Prince Vladimir, do you think there was any real belief in the Energy eaters?"

Fred shook his head, no.

"Tell me, young Fred," she continued after a pause while they drained their cups, "Is strawberry juice the favoured drink at Castle Marsh?"

Fred thought a bit, with a puzzled look that was more to do with the switch of subject than the actual answer. "Well, yes, Lady Nimrod," he replied, "Strawberry juice has always been the traditional drink, in all its variations, partly due to the excellence of our strawberries."

"But you do not have an export trade in either juice or strawberries, do you?" she asked.

"Is export selling to other people outside the

Castle?" Fred had heard the term but wanted to make sure he didn't make a complete fool of himself. The lady nodded, and he felt encouraged, rather than stupid. "No we only grow the right amount to support the Castle and a little in store for emergencies. As I said, we use our land for many crops; we have to be very careful with good fertile land. In fact my studies have been useful in ensuring we maintain the right balance between keeping the ground healthy and taking goodness out through crops."

"Very wise to work for sufficiency rather than profit," said Lady Nimrod, although Fred wasn't entirely sure what this meant, his line being natural philosophy rather than economics.

"So you do not bring in other types of drinks from other Castles even for celebrations?"

"I don't think so," Fred replied. "The first time I saw a Vex bottle was when Victor, the barkeeper at the inn of the Seventh Happiness, was drinking it."

"And you were not familiar with Wozna at all until then," confirmed Nimrod. Fred nodded. "Well, I wonder why you have experienced the Energy Drain then, although it does not seem as bad as most other places. Maybe it is spreading," she finished thoughtfully.

"How long has it been in other places and do you think there is a connection with Vex and Wozna? Or any other drinks?" he added.

"Let me tell you what I know, then what I surmise, and maybe we can philosophise over the true meaning."

The mid-day meal arrived, and Nimrod encouraged Fred to tuck in while he listened as she explained how it started.

"The first inklings of an energy drain were experienced about eight years ago. The first occurrences were mysterious power failures at the Inn of the Seventh Happiness, then these spread to other inns, and then to castles between them. Vexstein was affected quite early, as we were. I discovered though, that we were not the first. Sowerby, and its surrounding area, was almost certainly the first castle affected. This seemed strange to me. Sowerby is so far away from anywhere else. Although whether the Inn or the Castle was worst affected was never clear. I went there one summer and found it to be a nice place, full of friendly people, but then as Midsummer Day drew near they started behaving oddly, and the innkeeper suggested that it would be best for me to leave. 'Strange things happen here at Midsummer,' he said, and I must admit, there have always been rumours of hauntings and goodness knows what up there. I left, anyway. I had gathered the data I needed.

"Although, as I said, it arrived at Buckmore relatively early, it did not cause real problems until four years ago. Every time we had a major event with a great many people visiting, the power would give out just at the most inconvenient moment."

Fred moved uncomfortably in his seat, remembering

the King's Birthday Gathering.

"The same for Castle in the Marsh was it not?" she asked, and he nodded. "When I visited Cole, he said he did not have much of a problem. When I described some of our incidents, though, he allowed there had been more difficulty than he had wanted to say to an outsider. So proud - and rightly so, to manage on your own so well. But what I did not understand, what I still do not understand, is why Marsh should be affected at all since it seems to be the only castle in the lands that does not import Wozna - or Vex. Cole said one of his princelings was doing great things in designing new energy engines to overcome the problem, would that be your brother?"

Fred nodded, pleased both that his grandfather had recognised George's work and had praised it to Lady Nimrod.

"So I added that snippet to my store of information, and came home to advise that we become more self-sufficient ourselves. However, we had already increased our power supply from our own water system which comes through the high hills beyond, and that had contained the problem for only two more years. I knew we were barely keeping ahead of the demands on the system, so last year I set out in search of alternative solutions, much as you have now. And in much the same way, I found that my focus shifted to examining the causes of the Drain, not just finding stop-gap solutions."

Fred nodded; it was not enough to keeping solving problems that occurred, one had to think through the problem, find the causes and eliminate them. George had taught him that as a fundamental principle of good engineering. George always complained that the problem with most people is that they would rather add something to keep solving a problem than go back and prevent it in the first place. The concept particularly appealed to Fred, who would much rather spend time thinking of Why? than of How? which was more George's line.

Lady Nimrod went on to list the coincidences that she had found as she travelled from castle to castle. Nearly all the inns had started to import either Vex or Wozna or both about a year before the Drain started in their area. Castles had taken them on at different times but their energy sources were more diverse and the Drain became a problem for some sooner than for others. Peaks in the Drain seemed to occur whenever they were running short of supplies, and it was not always the same season in each area - some had their peak just before the Solstice festivities, others at seemingly random times throughout the year.

"Then one day I discussed it with a very large black and white gentleman who was interested in the same question, or at least so it seemed as we conversed over dinner at the Inn of the River Cottage." Fred looked up at her questioningly and she nodded, "Yes, Hugo." she said.

"Let me tell you of that evening and you can give me your opinion, since you have met him, but as a complete stranger, as you might say, whereas the rest of us have slightly more knowledge of his history. Slightly," she repeated, as if knowing him longer did not give you more information about him.

She described how she had arrived one evening at the Inn on her way back from White Horse to Buckmore, intending to stay the night. Normally she would take her meal privately, but this inn was attractively set by the waterside, it was a pleasant summer evening and there were few guests about. Moreover, the innkeeper had brought a message from Hugo to invite her to dine with him, since he had seen her carriage when he himself had arrived. They had talked about general things, the food, the wine, and the state of the grapes at Dimerie, his new business interest as a strawberry purchaser, the usual chitchat. She could not remember whether he had asked what she was doing travelling or whether she had volunteered that she was investigating the Energy Drain, but he had represented that he was also investigating it, and asked her what she had learnt.

"I told him of my information about the spread of the Drain and the impact it was having, and tried to get him to tell me more of what he thought of it, especially his experiences of it on his travels. At that stage, I had no concerns about sharing my information with him: he was well travelled, he had been to most of these places, and I expected that he had experienced the impact of the Drain himself. Much to my surprise, he had not, or else he maintained he had not experienced it. Now your grandfather had taken this line at first, Fred, but had quickly realised there was no shame attached to the phenomenon. Hugo seemed genuinely to have not experienced it. He then questioned me quite closely about my information, including how the Drain was coincident with the parties, gatherings or the need for a restock of supplies. He became quite defensive when I suggested there was a strange relationship between them. He practically accused me of inventing stories to discredit his business, implying that Buckmore's connection with Vex had coloured my judgement.

"And since that occasion he has hardly been seen in the region, unless it is to persuade another Castle to part with its strawberry harvest. He used to be around often when he first introduced Wozna to us. Now he only comes every six months or less, and a major Drain usually precedes his visits. Is it just coincidence? So when considering the problem of the Energy Drain, I have also been wondering what his role in it is."

She paused and looked at him closely.

"That is why I gave instruction that you should not travel with him, or even stay the night with him, just in case," she said.

Fred considered that. He had not felt any threat from Hugo, on the contrary, he had found him a most helpful and generous guide. If he was not what he seemed, was it possible that Lady Nimrod and Prince Lupin were also not what they seemed? What did she mean by 'Buckmore's connection with Vex'?

"The biggest coincidences that we need to consider,

Fred, are why Hugo is always around just after a major Energy Drain, and why localised Drains always seem to occur just before new stocks of Wozna are delivered."

Fred started to Think, but was interrupted by one more puzzle to Think about.

"And what are we going to do," posed Lady Nimrod, "when he arrives around sundown, which is just under six hours away."

Chapter 7: A Close Shave

In which George finds that engineers need people skills more than people need engineering skills

George's tummy rumbled very loudly.
"Oh, I'm so sorry!" exclaimed Saku. "We've been here for hours! When did you last eat?"
That was a very good question, thought George. Apart from a Wozna and a refined strawberry juice, he hadn't had anything since he left the castle on 2nd May 2009! He was feeling a little light-headed, but he was certainly ready for food. "I think it must have been yesterday," he responded vaguely.
"Let's go and get some good food then," said Saku, "not some of that fast food rubbish."
They went out of the laboratory and over to an archway in the corner of the corridor. Saku put a

hand on a pole in the middle of it and jumped onto it to hold on with his other feet, then slid out of sight. George peered down and realised it was a slidey pole. A bit tentatively, he followed suit. He enjoyed a very strange feeling as he whizzed down several storeys, of light-headedness combined with light-weightedness. He came to the bottom and stepped out, a bit wobbly, with Saku kindly helping him by the elbow. "I've never done that before," he gasped. "How do we get back up later?"

"I'll show you when the time comes," said Saku with a grin, looking like he had a real treat in store for George. "Come on, we'll go to my favourite diner." They set off into the dark world of Hattan, although with twinkly lights and shimmering glows from the buildings, it was no darker than most castles at night. It *was* night, thought George, peering upwards through the maze of towers. He caught a glimpse of deep blue sky, lit by the very last shafts of the setting sun. Past sundown, at any rate, he thought. The roadways were busy with people scurrying about, and the occasional carriage that moved without the need of draught animals. There were also strange carriages that moved on tracks. People got on and off them whenever they pleased, so it seemed, as there were platforms front and back. The carriages moved quite slowly as the people just wouldn't get out of the way of them fast enough. Saku called them 'trams'. He said they ran on cables powered by enormous wheels that used the wave and tidal power out in the bay.

They found a suitable dining place and sat at tables in the window so George could look out at the Hattanites as they went about their normal evening tasks. Most of them scurried about, but here and there he saw people lounging in doorways. He wondered what they were doing. If he looked directly at them, they looked away from him or seemed to busy themselves with something on the ground. It all fascinated him, so different from Castle Marsh. The menu came and apart from some dishes that Saku had to explain to him, he found it very understandable. There was a 'healthy eating' section which seemed to consist mainly of salads, and plenty of more international dishes. He selected an arugula salad to start with, followed by sweet potato and corn stuffed bell peppers with a side of zucchini, although he didn't recognise any of the vegetables' names other than corn. Saku went for the melon starter and the bell peppers too. The choice of drinks was interesting, and he decided to try a 'root ale' while Saku took a 'Superior', which he said was a brand of ale brewed up in northern parts.

They chatted about life and their experiences. Saku wanted to hear minute detail about life at Castle Marsh, whereas his own tale of emigration to Hattan more than thirty years ago was equally fascinating to George.

"I left behind my beloved wife, and my lovely son," he sighed. "It was a heart-wrenching thing to do, but there were no opportunities for me, unless I went into one of the big industrial castles, and I didn't want to do that. With this post," Saku explained, "the opportunity was only available to single people, and my wife said I should go for it." He paused for a bit, and George noticed a little tear at his eye, which he wiped away under the pretence of tossing his hair out of his face.

"I bitterly regretted it, of course. I made sure she would be ok; I introduced her to a nice village and set her up with a little money for a market stall. I heard she settled again with a nice person that ran a prosperous business, and my son inherited it. But of course, that's a long time ago now. How do you like your dinner?"

George was enjoying the food mostly - he found that arugula was extremely like rocket, if not the same plant. Unfortunately, zucchini was rather like courgettes, which he didn't like, but no one seemed to mind him pushing it to one side, as there was far too much to eat even after his enforced fast.

"Shall we take the rest of this with us for later?" Saku asked. Much to George's surprise, the waiter carefully wrapped the food in shiny containers and put in a bag for them to bring back. "I'll put it in the cold store in the study area," Saku said. "Don't forget to have it for breakfast or any other time you fancy."

They took a detour on the way back to have a bit of a walk around the city. They sat on a park bench behind the library as the talk turned back to the problem of the time tunnel and the use of energy. "When did the time tunnel arrive?" George asked.

"How did you know what it was?"

"It was about six months after we went into full production on Diet Wozna," said Saku. "I was always a little worried that the two were related, but I couldn't see how that could possibly be."

George thought about it. If Diet Wozna really did produce an energy sink, using all this extra energy to reduce its own energy value from forty calories to one per can, then surely the stores of energy could be enough to power a time tunnel.

"Do you have any idea how the time tunnel works, or what triggered it into existence?"

Saku shook his head. "Afraid not," was all he said and looked glum.

"Let us hypothesise that the time tunnel is produced by the Diet Wozna production process," said George, thinking that phrasing it formally might help avoid any sense of criticism or feelings of sensitivity. "How could we test that?"

"Well, only by halting production, I suppose," said Saku, "And seeing what happened to the tunnel."

"Could we do that, do you think?" he asked, privately thinking that the chances of persuading Lord Mariusz to do that were rather small.

"Well, of course," said Saku. "Anything's possible."

They started back to the castle, keeping mostly to well-lit streets. Every now and then Saku said they would just nip down this alley or that to work their way across town. George thought he kept looking over his shoulder at something and wondered what was wrong.

Suddenly two guys appeared out of the shadows of a big box thing stuffed with rubbish. They rushed at George and Saku, bundling them into a very narrow dead-end alley that smelled of something nasty that had met its end there nastily. George fell on top of Saku as he sprawled on the ground. The two guys stood at the entrance to the alley facing them. One of them held a small tube with a sort of handle on it. "Don't shoot!" cried Saku as George got to his feet and the person holding the tube pointed it straight at him. "Here, take this, it's all we've got." And he threw the bag of food at their feet.

The guy not holding the tube laughed.

"We don't want your dinner, Prof," he said in a funny sort of accent, even compared with some of the people they had met in the dining hall. "Our boss wants you, alive! Who's the spare?" he added, nodding at George.

"He's a very important guest of Lord Mariusz's," said Saku quickly, thinking he'd better protect his friend's reputation. George was completely bewildered.

"Oh, yeah?" said the guy with the tube nastily. "Well, we've only room for one."

There was a loud bang and George dropped to the ground. Saku fell to one side and the guy with the tube fell backwards. At the same moment someone rushed through the gap between Saku and George and started hitting the first guy very hard, with sickening thuds and cries of 'oof' from him as the blows hit home. But then he rallied and turned his

assailant upside down and went to jump on him.
The new guy rolled clear and caught the first guy's
legs with his own as he turned, bringing him down,
and they rolled over and over, each struggling to
finish the other one off. They rolled into trash cans
that were stacked nearby and more sickening smells
filled the alley as the cans emptied their contents over
the already dirty ground. The newcomer caught
hold of the first guy's shoulders and started bashing
his head against the wall of the building at the side.
The first guy went limp and the newcomer stood up,
brushing the dirt off his coat, then walked to the
entrance of the alley and looked up and down the
street outside.

Saku got up and went over to George, who was just
watching, dumbfounded. He had never seen
anything like this before, not even when the kids
were playing in the castle square and squabbling over
a ball.

"Are you okay?" Saku asked, worry creasing his
already creased face.

"Yes, fine," said George getting to his feet.

Saku helped brush him off, although in truth there
was little to worry about.

"I thought you'd stopped a bullet then, when you
went down so suddenly," he said.

"What's a bullet?" asked George, which got a strange
look from Saku. He muttered something about 'tell
you later' under his breath.

The newcomer came back to them, eying George
with a sort of professional once over, and handing

him the bag of food retrieved from the ground.

"You might as well keep this," she said in a clear, sweet voice, "you might feel a mite peckish after your adventure."

"Thank you, Aurora," said Saku to the newcomer, who George now saw was a female person, neatly dressed in a dark suit, lithe and well balanced on her feet, like a dancer. "I'm always glad to know you're my security, and I always protest I don't need it, but I'm glad you were with us tonight."

"Nice speech, Prof. Just don't get into the habit of needing me. Okay?" and she turned and walked away into the night.

"She's gone!" said George, beginning to get some sort of idea of what was going on. "Who were those people that attacked us? What did they want?"

"Oh, they were just thugs from a rival castle," Saku replied lightly. "Lord M often says I shouldn't go out in case someone tries to steal me away from him, and so there's always someone, security they call it, keeping an eye on me. Just in case, you know."

"Good thing," George mused.

"Good thing indeed," said Saku, who appeared more shaken by the incident than he was trying to show. "Let's get home now though, it's not far and it'll be main streets from now on."

They chatted lightly about topics they had gone over earlier, trying to restore their balance and get over the shock of the assault. Saku explained about the tube shooting bullets out very fast and if they went into you they could do lots of damage to your body, as demonstrated by the way Aurora had shot the second guy just as he was about to shoot George. He wasn't going to shoot anyone else in future, that was for sure. Saku was amazed that George knew nothing about guns, as he termed them, but said it was a good thing really that people didn't use them in George's world as they caused a lot of problems, really. "More than they solve," he added sadly.

They reached the entrance to Castle Hattan safely. The guards at the entrance waved them through then locked and bolted some stout-looking doors after them. They were made of wood laced with metal of some sort and looked much stronger than the thick wooden doors of Castle in the Marsh, thought George. He wondered whether these other castles try to attack each other or whether it was just a show of superiority. Then he saw some stairs and remembered how high up the sky courtyard must be and his heart sank. He started towards them.

"No, it's ok, George," said Saku. "We don't have to walk. Come and try this."

He led George over towards the poles they had come down and demonstrated the use of some ropes that were hanging in an adjacent bay.

"It's all done by counterweights," he explained. "We can also restore some of the energy in the system by getting them to charge our dynamo too."

George had great fun with the counterweight system that lifted people up from floor to floor. Saku didn't mind letting off steam either, after their shock, so they went up a few floors, then came back down again laughing and chatting about their energy theories again. The guards at the entrance door watched them in partial disbelief and partial disapproval. They went right to the top, where Saku said they should have a look at the city by night, as well as the lovely stars.

As they walked to the arches to look down on the twinkling lights below, Lord Mariusz came out of the door leading to his quarters.

"Greetings, my lord," said Saku, and George echoed him and added a formal bow for good measure.

"We've fixed the power supply and had some ideas we'd like to discuss with you."

"I'm kinda in a hurry. Give it to me in a nutshell," Mariusz responded.

"We could test our theory on the time tunnel if we can put production off-line for a day or two," said Saku.

"Not exactly off-line," put in George hurriedly, "we can keep production quotas well in line with target."

"WHAAT" said Mariusz, "What the h--- do you think you guys are playing at?"

"Well it's only..." started Saku, but Mariusz interrupted him.

"I have to go - now" he said, as the clock on the tower as it started to strike midnight. He dashed into the time tunnel.

"Oh well," said Saku, with a sort of sag to his shoulders.

"I don't think you should have put it in a nutshell," said George sadly. "I generally find you have to be very cautious about explaining these sorts of things to people. They usually get the wrong end of the stick."

Saku looked crestfallen. "I suppose you're right," he said. "It's why I try not to talk to people really."

They turned back to the view, both wrapped in thought. George was divided between wondering about the source of the time tunnel and wishing he could ask Fred to Think about it. Saku pondered the impossibility of persuading people to his point of view.

Suddenly Mariusz rushed back out of the time tunnel, his hair dishevelled and with dirt on his legs and feet.

"YOU!" he yelled at George, who sidled off to the right in order to avoid a direct confrontation.

"AND YOU!" he yelled at Saku, who edged off in the opposite direction. He strode over to Saku and cuffed him round the ear: "I've a good mind to throw you in chains!"

George, who didn't like the sound of this at all, continued to edge round so he was well away from the action. He wished he were in his own castle where he knew where the secret passages were to provide easy exits.

"And as for you, you meddling, interfering, jumped-up little nothing...." George continued to edge sideways as Mariusz started towards him. "YOU will be locked in chains and thrown into my deepest dungeon. GUARDS!"

At the sound of that, George ducked under all the

outstretched arms that suddenly appeared to try to grab him, and jumped down the only secret passage he knew... the time tunnel.

Chapter 8: Food for Thought

In which Hugo gets into a Lather and Fred takes a Philosophical View

Fred was gazing from a window once more. Behind the sheer drapes, the window looked onto the whole world, or so it seemed. Whereas the other arches looked over the courtyard garden, these looked from the highest side of Buckmore Crags. They had excellent views both back to the river crossing and the other way to the mountains, now bathed by the late afternoon sun. Some movement on the other side of the distant bridge caught his eye. He called to Baden, who was sitting drinking tea and doing his crossword again. They agreed the carriage was returning, and set off back to the plaza near the entrance.

It had been an exhausting afternoon. After an hour or so of hard Thinking, Lady Nimrod had called them back together to exchange ideas. They had not thought of any useful, concrete solutions, but they generally agreed that the Energy Drain had to be connected with Wozna Cola, and it was possible that the delivery of cola was intimately linked with the Drain. How to test this they had no idea.

They had more success discussing what Hugo knew about it. If he did know about the connection, was it was deliberate or unintentional sabotage of their energy system? In either case, what would he do about it?

The big question was whether it was possible to discuss the issue with Hugo if they had not proven that the two really were connected.

"There are sufficient lines of co-incidence, surely," Baden said.

"It still could just be co-incidence, though," said Fred.

"I agree," said Lady Nimrod. "It might be an effect, but is it the cause?" She looked around at them. "Well, what shall we do about it?"

They finally agreed that Lady Nimrod would speak to Prince Lupin and together they would tackle Hugo about the co-incidence, and perhaps see if he had noticed anything on his travels that could account for it.

Now Fred and Baden stood in the plaza listening to the carriage making its manoeuvre up the passageway.

"It looked very much like the carriage we came in," observed Fred as they waited.

"It is the same one," said Baden. "I sent it back for them to change into at Castle Powell, where they would have stopped for a late lunch. My animals aren't up to such a long journey, and they're much slower than Lupin's anyway. It looks much better if he arrives in his own coach as well!" he added with a grin.

The carriage emerged from the darkness, and first Prince Lupin, and then Hugo emerged from the carriage. Prince Lupin looked immaculate as always and greeted the people around him in a friendly manner. All were very pleased to see him. Hugo, in contrast, looked rather less than well groomed, although he did his best to look suave and sophisticated as usual. He had a slightly fractious air about him.

"Welcome back," said Baden to Prince Lupin.

"Thanks for thinking of sending the carriage back," he replied with a grin. "We would have taken hours more with those slowcoaches of yours. Ah, Fred, you made it ok, then. How's your day been?"

"Very good, thank you, sir," Fred responded. He noticed Hugo give him a very odd look. He wondered what Hugo had thought when he woke up and found Fred missing.

"Baden, would you show Hugo through to his rooms? I think we'd both like to freshen up before dinner." As Baden led Hugo off, the Prince turned to Fred and bade him walk beside him.

"I think Lady Nimrod would like to talk to you, sir,"
Fred said, checking that no-one was close enough to
hear him.

"Yes, let's go there," Lupin replied. "And tell me
what you two have been thinking today. I hope it
got you somewhere."

"We have a plan, sir," he said, and with
encouragement that the lady would not mind him
explaining, Fred told the Prince of their conclusions
as they walked.

They entered Nimrod's apartments and Fred watched
an affectionate greeting. He wondered what the
relationship was: were they friends, siblings, cousins,
lovers? He couldn't tell. It was affection between
two caring people who had known each other a long
time.

"Now, let me tell you some curious things that
happened after you left the inn," Lupin said to both
of them. "I had been up before dawn as arranged,
since one of my people wanted me to check
something about Baden's carriage. Hugo appeared
from a tunnel, running towards the inn. He saw me
and proceeded to do some stretching exercises as if
he'd been out for a run."

"Sorry I'm late, your highness," he had said, "lost
track of time a bit."

"I told him we were ready to leave and checked
whether he needed anything from his room. He said
he'd got everything with him, but could do with
freshening up, so I passed him a towel from the stack
my people have and we settled down in the carriage.

He was very quiet for a long time, and I dozed a bit. A while later, we'd passed the halfway point, I think, Hugo came out of what was obviously a solid piece of thinking, and asked where Fred was."

"Don't say the stupid lad has overslept!" he said.

"I reassured him that you'd been up early, Fred," Lupin said, nodding to him, "and so I'd sent you on with one of my princelings. Which of course is true, except that Baden isn't exactly my princeling," he laughed. "Other than that, the journey was uneventful. The breakfast basket was much appreciated, especially by Hugo, and lunch at Castle Powell fulfilled its excellent reputation.

"The questions are," said Lupin, "why did Hugo go out for a run, which doesn't seem to be the style I expect from him, and why such a long one as he was covered in sweat? And why didn't he notice that Fred had already gone from the room when he went for his run?"

"Maybe he crept out quietly so as not to wake me," said Fred.

"This may sound strange, but was he really there when you left?"

Fred paused, thinking back. "I heard him snoring, very quietly though."

"Ah," said Lupin, disappointed. "And do you think he could have gone past your bed without realising it was empty?"

Fred tried to remember the exact layout of the small, dim room. Although he could slip out easily, he was not so sure Hugo would not have stepped on him as he had when they retired to bed. Fred had kept quiet about it, and he didn't know whether Hugo had noticed. Maybe he wouldn't have noticed not stepping on him either. Lupin sighed as Fred explained this.

"Inconclusive, then."

Nimrod looked up and smiled at him. "It seems that everything our Hugo is involved with is plagued with coincidences. But if he had been out for a run even of an hour or so, surely he would have remembered Fred was with him before ... when did you say he asked about him?"

"About halfway to Castle Powell, so about 11 o'clock."

"That's an awfully long time to forget a companion," commented Nimrod.

It is a good point, thought Fred, "but I'd only been a companion since the previous, well, night or two, since the first was in the tunnel," he said.

"In my experience, Hugo has an eye for detail, and an excellent memory," said Lupin. "No, I think he forgot about you, and nothing immediately before this 'run' gave him cause to remember you. Something is on his mind. I wonder whether we can find out if he received any sort of message when he was at the inn."

"The innkeeper never mentioned a message when he was with me," said Fred, thinking carefully. "I don't think anyone passed him one, either."

Lupin sighed again. "But when he was with me any one of those scoundrels that mix with the genuine hangers-on could have slipped him a note or whispered something and none of us would have noticed."

"If they did, he hadn't read it or thought about it," said Fred. "He was perfectly well-tempered and very generous all evening."

"That is a very good point," exclaimed Lupin. "That is what is different! Something has happened since he went to bed and he came back to the inn this morning. He must have gone somewhere to find something out. Where did he go, and what did he do? And what was it that has ruffled his hair so much?"

"And how do we find out," added Baden, who had been listening at the back after showing Hugo to his rooms.

"Does this change our plan for Lupin and myself to discuss these coincidences with him, boys?" asked Lady Nimrod, referring to the plans hatched after their Thinking that afternoon.

They sat and Thought for a few minutes. In the distance, a bell rang, echoing through the corridors and courtyards.

"We need a quick decision," said Lupin, standing up, as Lady Nimrod moved to her dressing room dusting down her robe. "That is the bell for dinner. Wash hands, brush up, young Fred, we need to be on our way. Take your lead on this from me, everybody, please."

They hurried down to the dining room. A hundred candles provided a gentle glow for a relaxed yet formal dinner. Hugo waited for them at the entrance, looking his usual urbane self. Prince Lupin greeted him warmly and guided him to sit between Lady Nimrod and himself. Fred took the other place next to Lady Nimrod, much to his pleasure, and Baden sat on his other side.

Dinner proceeded in the manner of a slightly grander celebratory dinner at Castle Marsh where he and George were required to be present, with the exceptions that George wasn't there (and Fred felt his absence acutely by now) and the company was much more enjoyable. Even though Lady Nimrod spent most of her time attending to Hugo, Fred felt relaxed with the situation. He listened to their interchanges as well as chatting to Baden, when Baden wasn't engaged in deep conversation with a lovely young lady at his other side.

Hugo's charm had returned. He agreed with Lady Nimrod on the issue of the coincidences of the Energy Drain and Wozna deliveries, but suggested that the delivery vehicles had been fully charged at the depot and could have no influence on local power supplies. He turned to relating amusing stories, so Fred's mind turned to the question of his 'run' this morning.

He agreed with Prince Lupin that exercise was unlikely to have been Hugo's purpose. He was undoubtedly fit, but they had engaged in a fourteen-hour journey the day before. An hour's run down that tunnel was hardly likely to have been just for exercise.

It gradually dawned on Fred that as far as he could remember, apart from a couple of alcoves where they had rested for a few moments, there were no side tunnels and nothing else along that route. Either Hugo had gone back to the area he had met him, or he had gone to Castle Marsh. And he had done so, there and back, within a period of roughly seven hours. It was impossible.

Fred thought again. He had been tired near the end, so could he have missed something within the last three hours of their trek into the Inn of the Seventh Happiness? He tucked into the fourth course to have been set before him that evening, a delightful compote of strawberries garnished with mint leaves, and thought carefully. No, he concluded, there really hadn't been anything else because he had been looking for an excuse to stop. Hugo must have been to the place where he met him, or to Castle Marsh, in around three hours each way. That was surely impossible unless Hugo had some sort of time machine!

The candlelight reflected on the lavender sorbet, which now replaced the empty compote dishes. The memory of a strange light flickered into Fred's mind from the overworked memory. *Maybe he did*, he thought, astonished, and looked around him wide-eyed, remembering just in time not to look in Lady Nimrod's or Hugo's direction but instead concentrate on Baden's side.

"Are you all right old chap?" murmured Baden.

"I've just had a breakthrough," he responded, just as

quietly. "Give me a little while longer to think about it."

"We're on the last course," said Baden, "so carry on while the sweetmeats do the rounds and then move over to the balcony when we disperse. Tell me then."

Fred nodded, then caught himself wondering once more who to trust. If only he had George to talk to! Meanwhile, what were the implications of a time machine? He'd read a book or two that involved time machines in the Castle library. They were very tricky things. Answers came flooding into his mind as he walked slowly over towards the balcony.

A time machine would require huge amounts of energy.

A time machine could mean Hugo was from the future - and probably so was Wozna Cola.

A time machine was an impossibility - wasn't it? But if it wasn't....

Maybe it wasn't a case of *where* was George, but *when* was George - and was he in danger from Hugo?

"Urr, hi, old chap," said a smooth voice behind him. "What happened to you this morning, then?"

Chapter 9: Relativity

In which George gets his lines crossed and asks a Vexed Question

The light was whirling all around him again. George felt himself lifted off his feet and whooshed around; he felt like an autumn leaf tossed in a storm. His stomach felt all funny and he clenched it to stop it feeling quite so bad. He landed not quite on all fours on a nice earthy smelling tunnel and he rolled over a couple of times before finding his feet.
This must be the tunnel from Castle in the Marsh to wherever Fred went, thought George. *The one I've fallen out of is the time tunnel one.* He turned carefully and sure enough, there was a little ring of lights, glowing faintly now they had done their job with him. He wondered whether anyone would

follow him from Castle Hattan. That idea alarmed
him a little and he took two steps down towards the
damper smell, the way home, before he realised that
Fred wouldn't be there. He still had to work out
what to do about the Energy Drain, and so it would
be pointless to arrive back at his home castle. He
turned around and started walking briskly up the
only tunnel he hadn't been along so far.

It was a long way.

It was very boring.

He imagined there was a funny echoing noise of his
footsteps that seemed to be getting louder.

It sounded more like running feet coming towards
him, and they weren't his. He pressed himself against
a wall. A large shape, possibly black and white
although he really couldn't tell that well in the
blackness of the tunnel (even his eyes weren't good
enough for that), rushed past him and disappeared
into the distance.

George stepped back into the main corridor and
continued on his way, puzzling over this event. It
didn't take him long to work out that it must be
Mariusz heading back to Castle Hattan where he
would arrive... when? How did the time tunnel
work? What were the rules of time travel? What
governed the time you arrived at the other end?

He plodded on and on, with only a few breaks when
he came to little alcoves in the wall. The lucky thing
was, he found himself still holding the bag with the
little trays of food from the diner, so he was able to
refresh himself at these stops with leftover stuffed

peppers. He still didn't like the courgettes, but he decided to keep them in case he got desperate.

After many hours and several rests, he could see a light ahead of him. At last, he emerged into a sunlit square with an inn in the middle that served lovely refreshing strawberry juice. He took a seat at an outside table at the Inn of the Seventh Happiness and rubbed his sore feet. It helped him take his mind off his journey here, and he thought he probably needed to empty it for a while before he had any further adventures.

People came and went as he sat there, nursing his drink and his feet. As he revived, he started to look about him more, enjoying the sunshine and the view. He recognised the signs of a couple of castles that were made by people that greeted each other, and a couple were flicked his way, in which case he returned his own, which always produced a welcoming smile from the other person, although they were usually in a hurry to depart. Three of the tunnel exits seemed particularly popular. No one went down the one from which he had emerged.

As the afternoon turned into sundown, he went indoors and asked at the bar whether it was possible to stay the night. The young barkeeper, who had been absent when George arrived, looked him up and down. "You wouldn't be George, would you?" he asked.

George was surprised, but he nodded, and the young person explained that Fred had been worried about him. Just then, a large carriage arrived at the staging post in front of the inn, and hordes of passengers poured in.

"I've got a room for you," called the barkeeper, as he became a whirl of activity serving everyone at once and allocating some of them rooms.

George picked up the refill of juice and returned outside, but it was noisy there. Workers were arguing, transferring luggage onto smaller wagons, buyers pushing small animals into cages squawkingly, and a few traders wandering around selling items like sweets and books for the journey to come. He wandered around the market stalls and looked at the clothing and fabric, and souvenirs of far off places. He looked through postcards of beautiful castles... none of Castle in the Marsh, he noticed, not surprised at all. There were three different views of Castle Vexstein and Castle Buckmore, and two of Castles Powell, Fortune and Dimerie, and about seven others with just one view each. He thought Buckmore looked very pleasant, a nice place to live; Vexstein looked very imposing, perched high up in the mountains but with lush fields below. The others looked like variations on the same theme as Marsh, but with different types of landscape around them. When he got back to his starting point the rush had disappeared; there were plenty of people in the inn and some people were eating. He looked through the menu and decided on the Melange Excel, and enjoyed the crunchiness of the mixture when it arrived.

Gradually the events of the last couple of days started

to creep back upon him, and he decided he needed to be somewhere quiet to work out what to do next. He went back to the bar.

"Er, please could I go to my room now?" he asked the barkeeper as he rushed past once more.

"Yes, sir. Be right with you. Any moment," was the response over his shoulder as he dashed in the other direction. Sure enough, it was only a few minutes before the barkeeper came back. He took him across the room and down a spiral staircase.

"Sorry about the rush. Always a busy time."

He led George into a small cubbyhole saying, "Your brother stayed here. I'll come back later - explain. Food good? Any more needed? Or drink?" and on receiving negatives to these last two, he dashed out. George lay down on the corner bed and allowed his thoughts to run free again.

He was reasonably sure that the time tunnel was caused by the energy sink caused by the production of Diet Wozna. There was too much spare energy flying around from that process. From what Saku had said, the time tunnel had appeared not long after they went into full production of it. But how was it connected to the Energy Drain - if indeed it was? Was that the effect the time tunnel had on this end? Why? What made the big power drains? Why didn't they happen all the time?

He didn't find any answers to these questions, so his mind drifted to the other events. Why had Mariusz been rushing back along the corridor? Had he had time to get here and receive news that needed instant

action? What time would it be when he got back to
Hattan? It seemed to be twelve years ahead of here,
but exactly what day and time? Would that be before
George's arrival or after his departure? George didn't
know much about time tunnels, and they were all
fictional or theoretical anyway. From what he'd read
there were plenty of conflicting theories. One of the
most important theories was about meeting yourself,
or younger versions of yourself. Some people
described it as a paradox, others that it couldn't
happen and still others said you would both explode
or something, as you couldn't be in the same place as
yourself at the same time. If that was the case, then
was the Mariusz who had run past him to get back to
Hattan going to arrive before George arrived or just
before he left?

George remembered how Lord Mariusz had both left
and returned to Hattan when George and Saku were
in the sky courtyard after their evening out. It made
sense if the Mariusz who thought he and Saku were
going to halt production to test their theory was
rushing back to stop them. In doing that, he had
caused George's own abrupt departure. George
wondered if Mariusz's visit here, to the east lands,
had given him some special information for whatever
was going to happen when he got back to Saku. Why
had it been so important for him to leave at midnight
instead of hearing them out, though?

How long after George had left Hattan would
Mariusz come back here?

These were all things George did not and could not

know unless he went back again. He thought about that. He then decided that going back would be the last thing he did. He did not want to face Lord Mariusz again. But how could he stop the Energy Drain without stopping the time tunnel? If he had to stop the time tunnel working, he did not want to be on the far side of it when it stopped.

And with that slightly uncomfortable thought, he fell asleep.

***

He woke with an irresistible urge to scratch his leg. He pushed the covers back and found the barkeeper tickling his leg with a feather.

"Sorry," he said. "Thought we should talk. Is it ok now? Brought beer!" and he gestured towards four bottles labelled Vex in green writing. He passed one to George, and settled down in a corner with another.

"What time is it?" asked George, although he didn't mind and was quite awake.

"About 4," replied the barkeeper. "Still dark."

"You knew my name. You met my brother," George said, thinking as he said it that this style of speech could be catching.

"Fred said your name. Left with Baden. Honourable man. Not Hugo he came with. Nice man, never been sure whether honourable," and he frowned and took a swig from his bottle.

George tasted the contents and found it very pleasing. "Was Fred ok? And what's your name?"

"Fred fine, well, safe. I'm Victor. Run this place for

my dad. His dad before him. My step-grand-dad."
"What happened to your dad?"
"Lost looking for Energy Drain."
"When does the Energy Drain happen, Victor?"
"Always when we're low on stocks. Expecting more.
Hugo usually knows. Arrives to check orders.
Always that tunnel. Only him. And now you. Only
ones to use that tunnel. Ever. Since early days."
George pondered that. He felt sure that their long
trek from Castle in the Marsh to the zigzag where
they first saw the light was the first use of that tunnel,
and in response to Fred's request. But only this
Hugo guy using it? Well, that was wrong as he'd
seen Mariusz use it, hadn't he? Well, he wasn't
entirely sure. But if Mariusz hadn't emerged in that
corridor from the time tunnel, where else could he
have gone? Two exits from a time tunnel sounded
highly dubious. This Hugo chap could be Mariusz's
local agent. Maybe Mariusz had to set up a meeting
with him in one of those alcoves.
"Where are Hugo and Fred now, Victor?"
"Castle Buckmore."
George remembered seeing the pictures of it on the
postcards. Should he follow? What did he actually
want to do now? Victor interrupted his thoughts.
"My dad took different tunnel. Castle Vexstein.
Where this beer's made. Heard of bad Energy Drain
there. First castle affected. Started with inns, later
castles."
"What's your dad's name?"
"Argon. Stepson of Neon. Established the inn

twenty years ago. But his real father was a mad scientist who fled to the west."

George's blood ran cold. Here it was 2009 and in Hattan it was 2021. In Hattan it would be thirty-two years since the inn was established, and Saku had said he had left over thirty years ago. It wasn't important if he was talking to Saku's long-lost grandson. But if he was it was yet another co-incidence. Could they really use those co-incidences about the time tunnel and the invention of Diet Wozna without testing their theory? Was he just jumping to conclusions? He drank his ale and accepted the second bottle that Victor offered him.

"When did you first start getting Diet Wozna here, Victor?"

"Maybe ten years ago, less. Hugo came with samples. Tasted good. People liked the change. Modern flavour like Vex. More choice."

"Did you have ordinary Wozna before that?"

"No. Hugo brought both. We stock both. Most prefer Original. Funny idea Diet."

George smiled. He agreed but he understood the Hattanites' concern with size having seen them going about their business in their native city. But it was another coincidence. There was no Wozna here before Diet was invented. Perhaps there was no route here. But then he thought again. Wozna had been invented long before 1999. Mariusz had talked about the drought of '55.

"Had you heard of Wozna before Hugo came with it?"

"Oh, no. We were honoured. First to import it.
From the West. Big success. New trade route, Hugo
said."

Well, George thought. *If my theory is right, it wasn't
here before ten years ago simply because no one had
shipped it here.* George was very hazy about
international trade, but he imagined moving tons of
bottles around would be expensive, and probably
hazardous. Did Mariusz shift them all through the
tunnel? Maybe there was another route?

"And Castle Vexstein was the first outside the inns to
be affected?" he confirmed. Victor nodded. "I think
I'd better go there," George said.

"Me too," replied Victor, giving George a surprise.
"Only two hours. Back for evening. Dad started
that way."

George smiled again. The company would be nice,
especially the grandson of Saku who might have
hidden talents. But why was Victor so sure he would
be back for supper, if his Dad had never returned?
He turned in again, and was asleep in moments.

Chapter 10: Castle Vexstein

*In which Victor shows a surprising grasp of
unreality and George is left to ponder the
meaning of life*

George puffed and panted as they climbed the
foothills under the bright noon sun. Above them,
the mountains towered impressively, but George
was relieved to see signs of the grassy meadow
levelling out and Castle Vexstein looming ahead past
Victor's ample behind. It had only been a half hour
climb up from the rich fertile plains and the tiny
village where the post bus had dropped them, but
George wasn't used to climbing hills. Victor was
setting a good pace since he was keen not to leave
the inn for longer than he had to.
They had the bus to themselves, which was very

useful as they continued their chat where they had left off in the early hours.

"I want to find who last saw Dad," was Victor's main aim.

"If he was trying to find the cause of the Energy Drain he may have found out something."

"I think he suspected Hugo. Not in a bad way. Just something to do with Wozna or Vex."

George sighed. "I think Wozna is right. I have to tell you what I've been doing, Victor. You can decide whether I'm mad or not." George told him something his trip to Hattan, and his theory that the Wozna process caused the time tunnel.

"You know about time tunnels?" asked Victor.

"Well, it's only an imaginary thing in most books I've read," said George. "But I'm sure that's what I went through."

"When was the date there?"

"I think it was 2021. It seemed to be summer, early summer, but it's a busy, crowded place, and you couldn't tell from the land what season it was. It was hot though."

"Twelve years from now. Maybe the same month."

"Yes."

"And a black and white chap called Mariusz in charge?"

"Yes."

"Hugo is black and white. I was small when he first came. Maybe eight years ago."

"And he sold Wozna for the first time?"

"Yes. Him and Willow. Willow disappeared soon

after. Sold Wozna to us, other inns, then the castles."

"Who's Willow?"

"Just a chap. Not important. He disappeared."

George thought for a moment, but decided to concentrate on the Energy Drain.

"When did the Energy Drain first start?"

"I don't remember. A while later. Long after the fire. Not that long. Maybe a year."

"You had a fire?"

"Yes, the inn caught fire. I watched from Willow's office. Lots of flames. Scary. Dad rebuilt the inn. Energy Drain after that. Dad had someone check the building wasn't faulty. It was ok. Then other inns had same problem."

"So, as far as we know, Hugo brought Wozna to the realms, and about a year or two later, you had the first Energy Drain. Then the other inns, then Vexstein. What about other places?"

"Yes, they followed too."

George thought it was too much of a coincidence. Victor wasn't likely to know where Hugo had taken Wozna when he started selling it, but it sounded like the Energy Drain had followed him.

"Do you think it was this Hugo chap in the tunnel that ran past me?"

"No-one else uses that tunnel."

"I wonder how long it would take him to get from the inn to the time tunnel. It took me hours, but I wasn't running. Maybe twelve hours, or even longer if the time tunnel took me through at the same time as I jumped into it. That was midnight, and I arrived at the inn, oh, lunchtime, early afternoon?"

"If you run fast, maybe take half the time as walking," Victor suggested. "So Hugo takes six hours to reach the time thing. But he was back to leave with Prince Lupin. Maybe seven in the morning, he left. Didn't have breakfast. Took a hamper."

"And he definitely left with him."

"Oh yes. Gandy said so. He does early starts."

"So he couldn't run all the way down the tunnel and all the way back in time. Not in seven hours or less."

"Maybe Mariusz met Hugo in the tunnel. Then used time tunnel back to accuse you of, whatever it was he was going to accuse you of." That was a long speech for Victor, George thought with a smile.

"Maybe the time tunnel doesn't just send him back," Victor continued, imagining how it might work.

"Maybe it sends him back to just after he's left Hattan. Maybe it doesn't matter how long he spends here."

"So Mariusz arrived back with some information from Hugo? Just after he'd left to go at meet him? It's a good idea."

"How will we find out?" asked Victor. "Oh, we're here," he added as the coach stopped at a hamlet at the foot of the mountains.

As they walked up the steep grassy slopes, all covered with mountain flowers, George thought that Victor was probably right, and something was niggling him that he knew would confirm or at least support that.

The other thing that George principally thought was, for someone who kept a bar, and didn't exactly talk the most flowery talk in the world, Victor had a very good brain. Another point to confirm his theory that he was Saku's grandson, he thought, but kept these thoughts private.

They arrived at the entrance to the Castle, which was very impressive, with iron studded doors and a moat and a drawbridge. However, George did notice a set of modern doors further round the castle labelled "VEX BREWERIES - Deliveries and Wholesale Enquiries." That suggested Vexstein was a mixture of highly developed technology and strong traditions, although that might just be the façade. They went through the entrance then through the town that surrounded the castle, then up again to another imposing gateway. George was just beginning to wonder what they would say to any guards or butler, when a small door set in one of the huge ones opened and Victor engaged the doorkeeper in conversation. They both looked at him once or twice, and then the guard/butler nodded and waved them in.

"In luck!" said Victor, "Lord Darcy holding summit on Energy Drain. You're the Castle Marsh delegate. Many days travelled."

They followed their escort through the gates into a cobbled square then across and up stairs to a great wood-panelled room where about thirty delegates were already assembled.

"Baron Darcy of Vexstein, Lord Smallweed, may I

present to you Princeling George of Castle Marsh,"
said Victor as they were brought forward to meet two
imposing gentlemen, richly attired, who bowed and
smiled at George's formal response.

"Thank you, young Victor," the taller one replied.
"Won't you stay for refreshment? The meeting
recommences at 2 p.m."

"Thank you, Lord Smallweed." said Victor, again
losing all his mannered speech in the presence of the
Great. "Please may we recount some of our theories
to you in the interval as I cannot stay so long and
Princeling George would not wish to bore the
meeting with issues already discussed this morning."

"Very well," said Lord Smallweed. "Wait in that
alcove over there and we will join you."

"What should I tell him?" said George, slightly
panicked at all this formality.

"Ask what said this morning. Then tell what doesn't
know," said Victor, seating himself in the alcove,
which enjoyed a fine view over the meadows with
mountains to one side and plains to the other. They
both tucked into a plate of finger food they had
somehow acquired in their passage across the room.
They were joined by Lord Smallweed and another
chap he introduced as Pogo. As Victor planned, Lord
Smallweed summarised the morning's events, the
extent of the Energy Drain, reports from each
delegate on their attempts to overcome it, and the
ridiculous suggestion that it was somehow connected
with imported cola. "I have to say it was not a
suggestion supported by our family," Lord

Smallweed assured them "We have no wish to place any trade barriers and of course we are open to accusation of distorting the competition." George's heart sank. He hoped he wasn't going to have to talk economics with these people. It really wasn't his field.

"The co-incidences are mounting up, though, my lord," he said when it was appropriate. "In all our studies of the process, it would seem that the energy requirement for de-calorisation would lead to a substantial drain on the system." He hoped it didn't sound as ridiculous as he thought it did, as he was in no position to reveal his true thoughts yet.

"What evidence is there?" asked Lord Smallweed. George thought quickly.

"I have checked and modified a number of machines involved in the process," he said, more or less truthfully. "We would like to persuade the manufacturers to take production off line for two days in order to make the final test, but of course, as you know, continuous production is more cost-effective and they are reluctant to do this."

Memories of Mariusz's call for him to be thrown into the dungeon helped him to remember just how reluctant they appeared to be.

"You've actually seen the production lines?" asked Lord Smallweed, astonished, and the person called Pogo shifted uneasily beside him.

"Um, yes," said George, wondering how he was going to get out of this one.

"I'm surprised. They are the most secretive

organisation. Hugo is very good at not answering questions."

"Unless, of course, Castle Marsh is the centre of the operation, my lord," interposed Pogo. "After all, we rarely meet representatives of Marsh, and this must be a first for an official summit."

"I can assure you that Marsh is not connected with Wozna Cola in any way, my lord," responded George quickly, "save that our latest transport route seems to have inadvertently joined onto their own tunnel, which is a bit embarrassing." He hoped that would do. He knew that he needed help from some important and influential people in order to deal with Lord Mariusz and solve the problem. He really did want to be able to trust these people enough and gain their trust so they took him seriously.

"In truth, Lord Smallweed," interrupted Victor, "We have a theory that the trade in Diet Wozna is directly related to the Energy Drain, and we need your help to find a new trading system for them to use that will allow them to abandon Diet Wozna and use normal channels openly for the import of Wozna Cola itself."

They all stared at Victor, astonished. George kept his face still but inwardly he felt like crawling into a hole somewhere and hiding. He was about as tactful as Saku!

"I don't know what tittle-tattle you have been hearing at your bar, young man," said Lord Smallweed sternly, "but I advise you to return to your trade and keep your theories to yourself." A bell tinkled at the far side of the room. He rose. "Time for the summit to re-start. Thank you for coming, Princeling George, but I wonder whether you really have anything to contribute to the discussion," he said. He turned to an aide and muttered something under his breath, and the aide came and stood very close to George. He wondered if they were going to throw him into a dungeon. Lord Smallweed walked away, to be waylaid by one of the other delegates as he reached the halfway point.

"Sorry," mumbled Victor. "Thought should be direct."

George sighed. "Not your fault," he said. "I don't know how we can really explain all this - it sounds so ridiculous."

"I specialise in the ridiculous," said Pogo, who was still behind them, which they hadn't realised. "Why do you think that trade in Diet Wozna is directly related to the Energy Drain?"

George looked him in the eye and weighed up the consequences of trusting a complete stranger for the second time in a few days.

"Because we think the process has caused a time tunnel which is the way he's bringing it from the future to us," he said, very quickly in order to get the madness over and done with as soon as he could. "The time tunnel drains the energy from both timelines and they have more energy than we have. Wozna is ok, and has been manufactured for years, but Diet is causing the problem and must be stopped." He closed his eyes, hoping he wasn't going to be slung in a dungeon or thrown out on his ear, or, even worse, laughed at.

He opened them again as nothing happened. Pogo was looking at him with pursed lips, and as the moment went on, another aide walked up to him and gave him a message. He read it and pursed his lips even more.

"Wait here," he said and strode off after Lord Smallweed. They could see him showing him the message and discussing it, occasionally throwing glances their way. Their guard just stood there solidly, making sure they didn't escape or cause some sort of havoc in the lavish surroundings.

"I go soon," whispered Victor to him. "Catch next bus back"

"If we're let out," said George, and then added: "Yes, go if you can. If they let you out you can get a message to Fred at that place he's gone to, can't you?"

"Buckmore, yes," Victor nodded. He started edging away from George, and then stopped. "Guard said my dad went away with Hugo." Then he took a few steps to the side and slipped through the delegates who were milling around trying to get one more drink before they went back to the summit. George's guard let him go; he had only been told to keep an eye on the princeling.

George turned back to the window and looked out. He'd come all this way, he was more and more sure he understood both the problem and the solution, but he hadn't the faintest idea how to convince people he was right. The room grew quiet behind him. He sat down at the window and gazed out, looking much as Fred did when he was Thinking. After a few minutes, Pogo returned and sent the guard off to do other duties.

"H'hmm," said Pogo, understanding the need to dissolve someone's thought processes gently. "You may attend the summit. You will then stay with us to await the arrival of those who were previously unable to attend in person. Please do not mention your theory to anyone until they arrive."

And with that, he escorted George to a position at a long polished table in the next room, where all the other delegates were already settled and shuffling their papers. He found himself seated between Pogo and Lord Smallweed, where they could obviously keep a very close watch on him indeed. Pogo placed a set of papers in front of him, with the uppermost headed 'Agenda', and then placed the message, unfolded, just to the side of his own papers in such a way that George could accidentally-on-purpose read it. He tried not to be nosey, but noticed it was signed "Lupin of Buckmore", so he read on.

Chapter 11: Messages

In which Nimrod gets a message and Hugo jumps to conclusions

Fred turned to face Hugo with a smile on his face. "I'm glad to hear you didn't miss me till later," he said, still smiling. "I tried so hard not to wake you up when I decided I couldn't sleep any longer. A touch of excitement I think." Hugo continued to look at him, also smiling, but it didn't reach his eyes. "Have you heard about your brother at all?"

"No, I don't know whether that barkeeper would send a message if he turned up. Do you think he would?" Fred asked, suddenly anxious that he hadn't been worrying about George at all.

"Probably. He's a reliable sort, that Victor,"

said Hugo, and he turned to lean on the balcony beside Fred. "So, how early did you get here?"

"Oh not early at all," said Fred, rapidly thinking of what time he might have left the inn if they hadn't got to Buckmore that much before Hugo and Lupin had. "Well, I suppose we left well before sun-up but it was already broad daylight when we came out of the tunnel." Well, past dawn, he thought to himself, so he wasn't actually lying. He thought of saying something about Baden having to get back early, but decided that saying less was probably better, then he couldn't be caught out as easily. "Did you sleep well?" he added.

"Like a log," said Hugo and it was Fred's turn to smile without it reaching his eyes, as he sure that Hugo's sleep had been far from log-like. "You told me on our way to the inn that George was an uncommonly good engineer."

"Yes, that's right," said Fred, a little puzzled.

"Has he got any specialism? Energy, for instance?"

"Um, I don't know," said Fred, thinking he'd better be cautious if Hugo wanted George's skills for some particular purpose. "He's very good at working out how to test my theories and most of his machines use energy, but I wouldn't say he knows an awful lot about it."

"I've not been to Castle Marsh," said Hugo, apparently changing subject. "Do you do a lot of manufacturing?"

Fred thought for a bit. If Hugo wanted George to do something about his manufacturing, should he praise him or play his talents down? "Nothing on a large scale," he said, deciding on a compromise. "We only make enough to satisfy the needs of the Castle and its immediate surrounds." He had a vague feeling he'd said that before, but couldn't remember when.

"And what about making energy?"

"Well, we have water-power of course. And the pulley systems. George is working on a couple more ideas though." Why was he asking that, Fred thought, and then smiled to himself. "Why do you ask?"

"Oh, well... Seems to me, all the castles make at least some of their own energy. Maybe your energy drain is connected to your supply method somehow."

He continued asking about Castle in the Marsh, how many people were there, what they did, the land around, how far it was from the next nearest castle. Fred responded honestly and in a friendly manner, but he tried not to reveal more than necessary. He had never thought he was much good at what they called 'small talk', but he thought he acquitted himself well, especially by turning the conversation to Castle Wash.

"Have you been there?" he asked Hugo.

"Well, yes, I may have been," was the response.

"It's a great place, right on the sea wall," Fred continued, "with living areas and inns outside the castle walls themselves. What is the name of the inn there, now?" and he looked at Hugo, puzzled, as if trying to remember.

"Er, that is the Cheeky Parrot, I think," Hugo replied

with a smile, at first as if he thought he was being tested, and then it became a real smile, because he remembered he had good memories of it.

"What do you think of the place?" Fred asked with a smile, encouraging him to talk some more about it. He'd never been there, but had met a number of the messengers, so he had a vague idea of the place. By making up things and repeating what they'd told him over firelight tales at his own castle, he kept the conversation focused on Wash for a good few minutes.

He was relieved when Baden joined them. And interested at his relief; he had obviously decided deep down inside whom to trust. The conversation turned back to the meal, the gathering, the conversation, and Hugo's witty stories.

"I'd love to be able to tell those sorts of tales the way you do," said Baden, so naturally that it hardly sounded like flattery. "But you are skilled at working with people in your role anyway." Hugo nodded. Baden continued: "Prince Lupin was wondering whether you would like to go for a run with him in the morning. He doesn't often get willing company. I hate running!" and he laughed. Hugo looked a bit cross. "Well, I would of course be flattered to accompany the Prince on a run at any time. What time do you think we should meet and where?"

"I would check with him when he comes over, he's doing the rounds at present and will probably join us soon, but I imagine he'll be ready around 7 a.m."

Hugo continued to look less than pleased but then visibly made an effort. "It will be a pleasure. It looks like it'll be a nice morning," he added, looking out at the sky.

The arrival of Lady Nimrod and Prince Lupin saved them from making further small talk.

"It's a lovely night," said Lady Nimrod, "Did you enjoy your meal, young Fred?"

Fred agreed he enjoyed his meal and praised in particular the lavender sorbet, saying it was both delicious and stimulating. Lady Nimrod managed to get Hugo looking charming again and they talked some more about the other guests and things that had been said to them on their journey round the room after the meal. Eventually Prince Lupin offered Nimrod his arm and escorted her from the room, and the guests dispersed around the castle.

Baden walked with Hugo and Fred back to their rooms. "We will breakfast together at 10 a.m., although drinks are served in the morning room from 7 if you wish," he explained. "I hope you enjoy your run, Hugo," as he left him at his quarters, receiving just a civil "Good night" in response, and then Baden took Fred not back to the room he had been shown earlier as his quarters but to another apartment on the same level as Lady Nimrod's.

Prince Lupin was waiting for him. "Sorry to keep you from your bed, Fred," he said, "but Baden says you've had an idea which we should explore tonight rather than waiting." He waved him to some comfortable-looking cushions and an attendant

brought some strawberry juice as well as wine. Fred
decided that as he had only sipped water at dinner he
might as well try the wine. It was the best he'd ever
tasted, he decided.

"So, what's this idea you had over the lavender
sorbet?" Prince Lupin prompted Fred.

"Well, let me take you back to how I met Hugo. I
was walking along this tunnel, already hours from
Castle in the Marsh. There was a double bend in it,
and then I could see a glow ahead. It came from a
side tunnel. The glow became a bright light, then
Hugo stepped out of the tunnel from the light, into
my tunnel, and the light faded to a glow. Hugo and I
spoke and we walked up the tunnel towards the inn
together. It took hours."

"Hugo appeared from this light, which disappeared,
you mean?" confirmed Lupin.

"Yes. The thing is, I thought of Hugo running down
that tunnel and running back again. He was still in
the room when I left with you," he said, looking at
Baden, "and he was running out of the tunnel when
he met you at about seven."

Lupin nodded, "that's right."

"Well, where did he go? There was nothing he could
have run to down that tunnel. Did he just go down
there for up to three hours, then turn round and
come back? It doesn't make sense.

"There was no reason for him to check out Castle in
the Marsh, and even if he did, he couldn't have
reached there in seven hours, even running really
fast. I took more than twenty-four hours without a

break, and Hugo and I weren't moving slowly." He stopped and looked at the others, feeling a little silly about his idea.

"Go on," said Prince Lupin, sipping his wine and looking at the colour of it, rather than at Fred. Somehow, that encouraged him.

"That light in the tunnel meant something. I think it was a machine or something that helped Hugo travel long distances. I think Hugo ran down the tunnel and got in his machine and went wherever he goes. Perhaps he wanted to find out something. Maybe, and I'm a bit worried about this, he wanted to see if George had used it by mistake, since he hasn't come up the tunnel to the inn. He asked me about George just now. I'm sure he knows something about him."

"I'm sorry, who's George," asked Baden.

"My brother. We left home together. He's a brilliant engineer. I was singing his praises to Hugo when we first came up the tunnel to the inn. I think he fell asleep when we stopped for a rest. He didn't catch us up, anyway."

"Hugo's machine. Where do you think it goes?" asked Lupin.

"I don't know. I just wonder, if he uses it to bring Wozna to the realms here, it must use energy. What if every time he uses it, the energy drain happens? Maybe it uses too much energy?"

"But how could Hugo get to his machine and get back again in time to meet me?"

Fred took a deep breath to steady his nerves. "What if Hugo has a time machine, or possibly the tunnel is the machine? He could go back to his time, or rather forward since he must come from the future. Then come back again at the time he needs to be here in order to be back at the inn to leave with you. If he really has to," Fred finished lamely. As mad as it seemed saying it aloud, his audience listened while he described the events.

"Why would he have to?" asked Baden.

"I don't know. I think it has something to do with George, though. The more I think about this, the more worried I am about him."

"Well, your hypothesis fits the facts," said Prince Lupin approvingly, "but of course it is only a hypothesis. How could we possibly test it? I will think on it and discuss with Nimrod in the morning. Perhaps enlightenment will arrive during my early morning run."

"Do you think Hugo will show up?" asked Baden.

"Surprisingly, yes I do," said the Prince. "It is worth his while to do so: he knows his bluff is being called. Don't worry too much about your brother. Hugo may be a rogue, but I've always known him as a kindly rogue." With that, he dismissed them and they returned to their rooms for the night, Baden kindly escorting Fred so he didn't get lost.

"I think you are safe here," Baden said to Fred as they neared his door, "but I will take the liberty of sleeping in the adjoining room if you don't mind. Call out if anything untoward happens."

Fred wasn't sure whether to feel slightly better or slightly worse at this announcement, but decided to take it at face value, and went straight to his bed. After a busy day that started early, he was asleep before he could have started counting.

* * *

He woke in morning sunshine with birds singing and a breeze waving the trees around. He stood at the window for a while looking out. Thoughts of yesterday streamed back into his consciousness. Was he being fantastical? *No*, he thought, *it is a reasonable explanation of the facts, as I know them.* Who was it who said, "When all the evidence is considered and all the impossibilities discarded, whatever remains, however improbable, must be the truth"? Well, it was something like that, anyway. He hadn't discarded all the impossibilities yet, but he was confident that he had got rid of a good deal of them. He got ready and went down to the morning room for a drink.

After a few wrong turnings and redirections by helpful people along the way, he found the right room. Baden was already sitting at a small table, drinking tea and reading a large flimsy book.

"May I join you?" he enquired politely.

"Of course," Baden responded, pushing aside some of his debris and pulling a chair closer.

"Do you know if Hugo and Prince Lupin went for their run?"

"I rather think they did," Baden grinned. "I was so pleased when I saw two figures off in the distance when I looked out first thing."

"It doesn't prove anything, though," said Fred gloomily.

"No, but it's nice to call his bluff. If he did run all that way he is certainly fit enough to run with the Prince," Baden said, and Fred nodded in agreement. "What do you think will happen next?" he asked. Baden folded his book and put it aside. "I rather think Lupin will push things forward in some way. There was a conference called by old Darcy over at Vexstein, which Lupin and Nimrod preferred not to attend, although they sent a deposition and a clear statement of their stance in any preferred action. If things change there we will hear from Darcy, or more likely Smallweed - by the way that's Baron Darcy and Lord Smallweed to you - and we will respond accordingly." He sipped his tea and gazed at the ceiling. "I wonder if the lady will make any changes after our discussions last night?" he asked it, clearly not expecting an answer.

It came from an unexpected route, however. "Yes indeed, the lady will make changes!" said Lady Nimrod, who was halfway into the room. "I have already drafted a message and am waiting for Lupin to return before asking you what you think, Fred."

"Me?" Fred said, startled into spilling his drink.

"You will understand, if it remains unchanged after I have seen Lupin," she said mysteriously, but with a smile. "Meanwhile I have sent a messenger out on an errand, which hopefully will mislead our possibly time-travelling friend." She poured herself a cup of tea from the ornate urn in the centre of the room and joined them, Baden going to find another chair after giving up his own for her.

They chatted for a while, but always watching for the returning runners. Eventually they could see two figures in the distance; Lady Nimrod rose.

"I will see you later, no doubt," she said, and she left the room.

Fred took his leave of Baden and returned to his room. A little later, a bell rang for breakfast, and he joined Baden, Hugo and others in the morning room once more. Prince Lupin joined them in due course. Hugo agreed that he had enjoyed the run, it was a particularly pleasant morning and that Prince Lupin was a fine athlete. Lupin in his turn complimented Hugo on his fitness and suggested he would make an excellent rugby player if he ever wanted to give up his work. Hugo smiled at this and made a polite comment about the achievements of the Buckmore team. Then he broadened the conversation to other activities by saying he thought cricket was more his line, judging from the games he'd seen being played around the country. Fred knew nothing of the game, and listened with complete mystification as Hugo and Baden discussed its social role in bringing different communities together, while Lupin excused himself, saying he had work to do.

After breakfast, Hugo suggested a turn about the castle. Baden and Fred got up to go with him, but an aide stopped Fred at the door to the morning room with a request to pay his respects to Lady Nimrod. Making his apology to Hugo and Baden, he found his way back to her apartments and waited at the door, uncertain whether to knock, call or what. Fortunately, an attendant came forward to enter bringing parchment and writing materials, and he was saved from embarrassment.

"Ah, good, Fred's here," remarked Prince Lupin. "Take a look at this draft, young Fred." He passed a large piece of paper to Fred. It listed the key issues of Hugo's behaviour over the last few years and especially the last few days. It noted their suspicions, and, whilst omitting any reference to time travel, made it clear that they were confident that the cause of the Energy Drain could be placed squarely on the methods used to import Diet Wozna. Furthermore, they asserted that Hugo was 'absolutely aware' of this impact. They also described George (here Fred made a few amendments) describing him as an engineer of consummate skill, who should be given every assistance by good men and true. They asked the Vexsteins to send immediate word of him should they come across him.

Fred handed it back, impressed. "What will happen now?" he asked.

"We'll send this off on the vacuum post which will only take an hour or so." Lupin replied. "I'll just do a handwritten covering note for Darcy and Smallweed to ensure it's taken seriously." So saying he seated himself and started a note which he signed "Lupin of Buckmore" with a flourish, and then he folded and sealed it. The attendant left with both documents and Lupin sat back, gesturing for Fred to do the same.

"And now we wait," he said. "What would you like to do?"

Fred suggested he might like to look around, and they decided that a small party might take a walk to one of Lady Nimrod's favourite spots, perhaps taking a small picnic basket with them.

Fred went off to find Hugo and Baden and give them news of the proposed picnic. He found them on the lower level battlements, above the entry plaza, looking down towards the river, and the idea of the picnic appealed to them even more than their previous proposal of a lunch table under the apple tree in the plaza. They took a side passage beside the main gate, going down a winding stair to the outside of the castle. Then they cut across the grass from the main track to join Lupin and Nimrod, and an attendant or two with the picnic things, who had come out by a different route. It was a pleasant walk despite the breeze, roaming over the meadows to a glade by a river, and Hugo and Baden discussed the merits of fly-fishing as they leant on a bridge over it, watching the trout swimming in the cool water below. Their peace was interrupted by a messenger running down from the castle.

"My lady," he gasped. "An express message has arrived from Castle Vexstein," and so saying he handed a rolled parchment to her. It was unfortunate that in the handing, he tripped on something, and the parchment went flying from his hands landing in a jumble, unravelling from its neat string. Sheets flew in all directions and the party scattered to pick them up. All seemed to be accounted for, and Nimrod sorted them into the right order and skimmed through them.

"Good news, on many counts," she said, "not least that your brother George is safely at Castle Vexstein, Fred. But they have need of our counsel and we must leave at once." She ordered the messenger back to the castle to make ready a fast carriage for five plus two attendants. They followed on, speedily but not hurriedly, and when they got back all was prepared for them. In rather less comfort than on the way there, as Fred was sandwiched between Hugo and Baden, although this did mean that he was facing Lady Nimrod and Prince Lupin, they seemed to travel at breakneck speed, stopping only for changes of horses.

In the tunnel that led to the Inn of the Seventh Happiness Hugo spoke. "I recall leaving something in our room at the inn, my lady," he said. "Might I take a moment to retrieve it when we change the horses there?" Receiving her assent, he settled back and relaxed again. Fred wondered what he had left. He couldn't remember that Hugo had carried anything with him when they had arrived. He didn't recall anyone giving him anything either. They stopped at the inn, where it was already dark, and Hugo left the carriage. Fred could see him speaking to the barkeeper, Victor. The horses were changed and Hugo had not reappeared.

"Where the devil is he?" snapped Lupin. "He knows

we're in a hurry."

"I shall check," said Baden going into the inn. He returned just a few moments later. "He's gone!" he said with a shocked look on his face. "Victor saw him running for his usual tunnel. Shall I run after him?" and he made to follow. Lupin caught his arm. "Stay, Baden. Whatever he's got wind of we will do better to go to Vexstein - we'll be there in 2 hours now, so let's not chase a will o' the wisp," and so saying he got in the carriage with Lady Nimrod, and Baden got in beside Fred, who moved across into the corner as they started off into yet another tunnel. Fred felt something scrunch up as he moved. He put his hand under him and pulled out a piece of parchment. It was a handwritten note addressed to Lupin and signed "Smallweed of Vexstein". He handed it to Prince Lupin.

"My dear and esteemed Lupin," he read out to the other three. "Notwithstanding the rest of the accompanying message, you should know most urgently that Princeling George considers it essential that we should cease importing Diet Wozna, which is principally responsible for the Energy Drain. We shall discuss urgently on your arrival. Wishing you a pleasant journey, etc., etc."

"The devil!" exclaimed Baden. "How did he get that? Had you seen it before?"

"No, I think he must have acquired it when the message flew open at our picnic," said Lupin in a very matter of fact voice. "The question is; what is he doing now?"

"He must be on his way to the time tunnel," said Fred. "I wonder if he will ever come back."

"Whether he intends to come back or not, my dear Fred," said Lady Nimrod, "is he hoping to stop something by his sudden departure, or is he trying to do something? And whichever it is, does it put your brother or any of the rest of us in danger?"

And the coach sped ever nearer to Castle Vexstein, while Hugo ran down the tunnel, not caring whether he ran into walls, or collected mud on his coat, just trying to get back as quickly as possible to prevent George leaving Castle Hattan.

Chapter 12: The Adventures of Victor

In which Victor gets more than he bargained for but finds that brains often skip a generation

At about the time the Buckmore party was pulling into the courtyard at Castle Vexstein, Victor was serving the last few customers in his bar and mentally counting the number of overnight guests he had. It wasn't many, as quite a few of those that had been hanging around earlier had departed with the delegates from Castle Vexstein's summit as they made their ways back to their own castles. Probably about half of the Baron's guests would have used the Inn of the Seventh Happiness as their crossroads. So while he had been hugely busy earlier, he wasn't now. And a plan was forming in his mind.

The one thing that he and George had not managed to work out was the time that the time tunnel sent you to, and whether the principle was the same at each end. What were the rules governing the tunnel? As the bar got quieter, he jotted down a few lines on a paper drawing them between East and Hattan, then scribbled them out, turned the paper over and tried again. Then found another piece of paper. At about the fourth go, and after the last people in the bar had either left or gone to their rooms, but it was still a few minutes early to turn in himself, Victor had a brainwave. It all hinged on George's understanding of what the person who rushed past him in the tunnel during his journey here from Castle Hattan was doing. What if the 'when' of it was wrong? What if he wasn't rushing back to throw George in a dungeon? If you changed those, a whole load of things fell into place. The two problems that remained were; did the time tunnel 'mind' if a person was in the same place at the same time, which was contrary to an awful lot of fictional speculation about the workings of time tunnels; and was Hugo the same person as the guy in Castle Hattan that George knew as Lord Mariusz?

George had assumed that the person who had rushed past him was Hugo or Mariusz on his way back to be cross with George and this Professor person he had called Saku. What if he was in a rush simply to be in a certain place at a certain time? If Hugo left his room to go down the tunnel to Hattan, but knew he would have to be back in time to meet Prince Lupin and set off to Buckmore, he would have at least a fourteen-hour journey but he only had about seven hours to do it in. The only way he could do it was if he could somehow overlap himself in the tunnel. If he knew he was going to do it before he set out, there should be no disorientation about meeting himself on the way back, as that was his intention. It would fit with the strange behaviour of Hugo when he had met the Buckmore party the previous morning. And now, this evening, he had come and said something very strange to Victor when they were changing the horses on the Prince's carriage for the final leg to Castle Vexstein. It didn't make any sense at all, but when Baden had come to find him, Victor had understood; he was merely trying to look as if he was talking to Victor, before slipping off down his special tunnel again. Giving the Buckmore party the slip, in fact. Victor wondered what had happened at Buckmore for him to leave them in such a sly way. He drew another line on his piece of paper. He and George had agreed the tunnel almost certainly originated in Castle Hattan, because that was where all the excess energy was made. If you left Hattan via the time tunnel, but always got back just a few minutes after you left (like this Mariusz guy returning just after he'd left George and Professor Saku), then you could spend a lot of time here and no time at all at the other end. If that was right, Hugo was just about to rush back with whatever information he had found out at Buckmore, and turn up a minute after he had last left... which would make him threaten George, and get George to jump down the tunnel. And that meant Hugo and Mariusz were the same person.

But George had arrived here in the afternoon after the earlier arrival of Hugo - the one where he had rushed to meet Buckmore's departing dawn coach. George had just taken more than twice as long to traverse the tunnel as he was in no hurry at all, so had arrived in the afternoon. He had passed the 'hurrying back after meeting Fred' Hugo in the tunnel. And that Hugo had passed himself a few minutes or maybe as much as an hour or more before he passed George, because of the one hurrying and George not.

George had then stayed the night and they'd gone to Vexstein together. It wasn't until Victor got back for the evening rush that Hugo had dashed down the tunnel because of whatever had happened at Buckmore. So whatever Hugo was just about to do to George had already happened, since George was back, and at Castle Vexstein. Victor frowned. Was this what they called timeline paradox? Would they all wink out of existence if Hugo, or Mariusz, as he should probably call him, managed to prevent George leaving, or was he merely carrying out something he was destined to do and he couldn't change it? Victor sighed. He couldn't quite work out when he would arrive on the other side if he went to Castle Hattan himself. It would be well after that event, he thought, as George's arrival in Hattan seemed to be in no way related to Hugo's previous visits.

Something itched in the back of his head. George had said something about his meeting with Mariusz. He said he'd been expected, or something like that. A light went on in Victor's brain. He was expected because Mariusz, or Hugo, had already heard of George from Fred on the way to the Inn. He had guessed that George might have gone the wrong way and ended up in Castle Hattan. He had dashed back down the tunnel, crossing with his returning self, and met George, who had solved his power problem! Victor drew some more lines on his paper. The time tunnel originated in Hattan, he thought. And that controlled when people would arrive in either destination. If you left Hattan, you arrived back more or less when you left. However long you'd been in the East. What if you started here? Maybe you arrived in Hattan a parallel time after the person returning to Hattan had left East? This is why Mariusz/Hugo had been expecting George. The number of hours that were between his and George's departure from East were the same number of hours between their arrivals in Hattan. Maybe. Victor frowned as he realised he might be going round in circles.

He looked up as the clock in the parlour behind him struck midnight. Hugo had dashed down the tunnel some hours ago. He would get to this time tunnel long before Victor would if Victor left now. But

George had said it had taken him more than half a day to do the journey, even though Hugo could run it in around seven hours, by their calculations. Victor couldn't be away so long, not with the inn to run. He sighed once more. His assistant called to him and said he was going. Victor nodded. Then he stopped him.

"Gandy," he said, "I need to go out on a mission. Tonight. Something to do with the Energy Drain. If I'm not back in the morning, could you and Missy hold the fort for me? Just till I do get back?"

Gandy looked worried. "You're not going to do a disappearing act like your dad did, are you?" he asked.

"No, I don't think so. I think I know what I'm doing. Just in case, I'll leave a note behind the bar. For Prince Lupin, or Baden. Or those nice young guys, Fred and George. You saw them, didn't you?"

Gandy nodded. "Mustn't let Hugo see note." Victor added.

They both agreed and Victor wished Gandy a good night and let him out, saying he'd see him tomorrow night. He turned the key in the door after him and stood leaning against the door. He did know what he was doing, he thought. He was going to rescue his Dad. It had to be why he had disappeared. If he had turned up at Castle Hattan sometime in the future, Hugo couldn't possibly have let him come back, even though they'd known each other and worked together since Victor was very young. It would have ruined Hugo's business forever. He wrote a short note to Prince Lupin and the others and placed in it the till. Then he went out of the back door, carefully closing it behind him, and into a little lean-to shed. He took an ancient cover off an equally ancient velocipede, wheeled it from the shed, threw his leg over the bar, and started pedalling down the tunnel towards the time portal.

* * *

At Castle Vexstein, the Buckmore party had met Lords Darcy and Smallweed in a small salon with a view of the mountains, where snow was twinkling in the moonlight. Although Fred and George were overjoyed to see each other again, they merely grinned at each other and sat down side by side, to listen intently as Lupin and Smallweed discussed the general situation. Midnight came and went before they agreed that it was the production and import of Diet Wozna that was responsible for the Energy Drain. It then took further long-winded discussion before they decided it was imperative that they should find Hugo as soon as possible in order to ensure that he ceased his import business. George shifted in his seat.

"Pardon me, my lords," he said, "But if we are to find Hugo, we may need to go down the time tunnel. And if we need to persuade Mariusz that his export trade and Diet Wozna are to be closed down, we need to have some good business alternatives for him."
And when we do close Diet Wozna production down,

he thought, *I want to be on this side of the time tunnel.*

All agreed that this was sensible. Lady Nimrod then rose and suggested that although we might think of some options for alternative trade opportunities, the problem was that Hugo's, or Mariusz's, trade options depended on being able to use the time tunnel. This was also agreed and everyone sat in silence for a while trying to think of a way out of the problem.

"Victor said that not many people drink Diet Wozna," said George.

"Perhaps we could look at bringing Wozna in through the normal trade routes in our own time," said Fred, almost as if George had continued speaking.

"Wouldn't that mean we changed the history in his own time?" asked Lady Nimrod. They all sat back gloomily and tried to think harder.

The clocks in the castle struck the quarters and then the hour of one. Lord Darcy looked up.

"We are making little progress," he said, "I propose we adjourn to our beds and sleep on it. Perhaps morning will bring new counsel."

They murmured agreement with him and went to their assigned rooms.

"I'm a bit too tired for talking," said Fred, "Although I'm dying to find out all about your adventures."

"I feel exactly the same," replied George, "and you seem to have had just as exciting a time."

And they laid their heads down and fell asleep without another word.

* * *

Victor had been pedalling for hours, he reckoned, and he wondered whether he had missed the tunnel. He remembered George had said it was the only turn-off, the tunnel narrowed after that and came to a zigzag, and he certainly hadn't had to negotiate a zigzag, so he just kept going. By his calculation, the velocipede would help him get down the tunnel at about the same rate as Hugo could run, so he shouldn't bump into him. The trouble was he had only his theory to work on as to when he would arrive at the other side relative to Hugo. He thought it would be either a few minutes, a few hours or as much as two days after him. He just hoped he hadn't left again in the meantime.

He was just thinking it was past his breakfast time when the tunnel narrowed and he felt a turning off to the side. He stopped, and carefully parked his velocipede on the far side of the tunnel that turned off. He could see a little ring of lights glowing faintly in the wall. *This must be it*, he thought. He stood at the edge of the ring, and took a deep breath. "Geronimo-o-o-o-o!" he said aloud, and took one big step forward. The lights came on, he felt lighter than a feather, and suddenly felt like he was whooshing through the air.

He landed on his feet and carried on walking out of a tunnel into a cloudy morning with a slight chill in the air. He looked around at the sky courtyard and felt slightly attracted to a particular archway, so without pausing to look at the view he went through it and down some steps. After a few moments he stopped, listening. There were footsteps coming towards him, not hurried, and a lot of breathing, as if someone not very fit was coming up the stairs. He suddenly realised he could hardly ask anyone he met "Excuse me, have you seen my father?" so he shrank into a convenient alcove and waited for the owner of the footsteps and the breathing to appear.

Round the corner came an old man, with rather wild hair, that looked rather like a mad scientist.

"Excuse me, young man," the mad scientist said. "Would you happen to know whether Lord Mariusz is up and about yet?"

Victor shook his head.

"Pity," sighed the scientist. "I was hoping to talk to him again about the supply of strawberry juice. Have you been in the castle long?"

Victor shook his head again. Definitely not long!

"So you don't happen to know where he keeps the key to the strawberry juice store."

Another shake of the head.

"Well, I could do with some help. If you are not on an errand, could you come along with me and we'll search for it?"

Victor nearly said something about looking for something himself, and then thought he might just as well go along with this gentleman, who was obviously looking for something, and it would be good cover for him, and he could do his own

searching at the same time. So he agreed and they set
off back up the stairs to the sky courtyard.

"What's your name, youngster?"

Victor introduced himself and learned he was talking
to Saku! He tried not to show how pleased he was to
have met someone he'd already heard of. He
wondered if he should call him 'Professor' or 'Saku' if
the need arose.

They went up and down a number of stairs, as Saku
seemed to be sure that the key was kept in a strong
room in a particular side room on the third floor
from the top. He just couldn't find it. They did,
however, find the breakfast room. They settled down
with a coffee and a twisted grain-cake for Saku, and a
plate full of carrot cake and maple syrup and
tomatoes and apple and a mint tea for Victor. Saku
gazed sadly out of the window in between watching
Victor demolish his breakfast.

"Time was I could eat like that," Saku said, imagining
the flavours of the past, "now I just have a little and
not often."

Victor carried on eating but behind him, people came
and went, with Saku occasionally nodding at them.
One person came in and Saku watched him intently.
Victor saw him looking and asked him who he was
looking at.

"I don't know," he said. "I've seen him from time to
time, but he reminds me of someone and I can't
remember who."

Victor turned round to see a person with a fine head
of red and black hair helping himself to some fruit

from the side table.

"Dad!" he said, standing up.

The person looked at him, astonished, then left his plate and came over to enfold Victor in his arms.

"Victor," he said, "how did you get here and why?"

"It's a long story - but why not get your breakfast and come and join us."

Victor's Dad did just that.

"Saku, this is my father Argon," Victor said. "He's who I was looking for."

"Argon?" said Saku. "I knew an Argon once, a long time ago. But you wouldn't be him, not so young. My Argon would be about ten years older than you."

Argon looked from Saku to Victor and back again.

"What is the year here, Saku?" he said. "I arrived by accident many months ago, and I never did work out the actual date."

"Why, its 2021, or is it 2022 now, I forget, never did keep much of an eye on the time." Saku responded.

Victor whispered at his Dad, "You can't tell him about the time tunnel."

"My hearing's quite good still, young man," said Saku. "I know all about the time tunnel, I've known about it for years. How do you know about it? Eh?"

"Um, I came through it just now," Victor said.

"And I came through it last year," said Argon, "and have been prevented from taking it back again."

"So, what's stopping you going back then?" and Saku peered at Argon, firstly through his glasses then he took them off and peered at him even more closely.

"Lord Mariusz, mostly. After he let me out of the dungeon he put me in, he got me to give my word of honour I wouldn't try to escape."

"Hmm, word of honour, wouldn't stop him, I don't think," muttered Saku.

"We'll have to persuade him to let you go then," said Victor positively. They discussed Argon's situation for a bit before Saku remembered he was supposed to be looking for the key to the strawberry juice supply.

"Why do you need it?" asked Victor.

"We have to top it up every now and then just to keep the power up. It sort of gets clogged up otherwise," replied Saku.

"And what happens to the production when that happens?" asked Victor innocently.

Saku looked at him sternly. "I don't think you need me to answer that young man, you are far too clever for your own good. Nearly as much as young George, but he had better manners."

Victor looked a bit abashed and decided to tell the truth. "We think we should stop Mariusz exporting Diet Wozna through the time tunnel. In fact, we think he should stop making it completely. How do you think we can get him to do that?"

"When George and I mentioned it the other day he was extremely angry. Extremely," said Saku, still stern like he was lecturing students.

"We need an alternative for him that will still make him rich," said Victor.

"There's more to business than that, m'lad," said Argon with a shake of his head.

"Not really, Dad. We have to find him a substitute product that will fill the gaps in his production line and income streams." They both looked at Victor for this long and involved sentence full of business speak. "I've been doing a course in business management by correspondence," he added, sheepishly.

"Hmm," mused Saku," You seem to have a good head on your shoulders young Victor. What sort of product do you think would work?"

"If we persuaded him to export just Wozna, then the energy expenditure on Diet would fall but he'd have more Wozna. He could export that and maintain the production."

"The only problem is, how would he export it?" said Argon.

"Can it be shipped by sea?" asked Victor.

"Maybe, if we could cool the containers for it. But the expense... " said Saku.

The three of them sat in silence, nursing their coffees and teas. Or in Victor's case, his empty cup, as he had long since finished.

"What if we persuaded Lord Darcy to export Vex to Hattan and on the return trip the ship would carry Mariusz's exported Wozna?" said Victor suddenly. The three of them exchanged glances. It seemed an ideal solution. If only they could persuade Mariusz of that.

"Let's go and see if we can speak to him then," said Saku.

"Before we do," said Argon, "I think I'd just better clear something up. Saku, are you my real father?"

A tear came to Saku's eye. "Yes, I think I might be," he said. "Especially with a grandson as brilliant as this," and he put his arm round Victor's shoulders and they started climbing the stairs back to the sky courtyard.

Chapter 13: A Question of Timing

In which Hugo (or Mariusz?) makes a pragmatic decision

Fred and George squeezed together to look out of the window. Their room was near the top of one of the towers, and it was larger than the cubbyhole that backed onto Uncle Vlad's fireplace, but smaller than just about anywhere else they'd lived. Baden had a room of his own just across the way, but otherwise they were alone. Princelings in Vexstein were not highly ranked; in fact, they were lucky they hadn't been put into a dormitory with all the family princelings, although they'd passed it on their way up to this room.

They had caught up with each other's adventures and were now watching the shadow of the morning sun sweeping across the plains as it rose higher behind the mountains. George reckoned it would take at least another hour to get to their window, by which time Prince Lupin would probably be back from his run and they could all have breakfast.

"I still think we ought to get Hugo, or Mariusz - do you really think they are the same person - to go for the ordinary export option. But the time tunnel won't be working, so how?"

George paused a bit before he replied, slowly as if still working something out. "He doesn't actually need the time tunnel to export to us; he would just be exporting to us in 2021 or whatever the year is. That would mean continuous production of Wozna, and no change in his income. The only people who would miss out are us, as we wouldn't have Wozna at all for, what is it, twelve years."

"That's no loss," they said in unison, and they laughed together. Then they just laughed because they were back together which made them feel they could do anything and it would work.

"It's a shame about that strawberry juice power though," said Fred. "It would be very useful and make up for all the drained Energy."

"Yeah, well, I could make a machine to run on it easily enough," said George, "but it would be using advanced technology from the future and I would endanger the timeline. Time's far too funny a thing to risk tampering with it," and he sighed.

They returned to gazing out of the window until they saw the figure of Prince Lupin coming round a crag on the mountain trail, headed back towards the castle.

"Good, that means breakfast in, what d'you reckon, twenty minutes?" Fred asked.

"Give him half an hour," replied George, but they got up and started to get ready all the same, and went down to the courtyard to see what was going on.

* * *

After breakfast, they were asked to gather in the room that had been used for the summit for the day before. As well as the Buckmore party there were some more of the Vexstein household, and a couple of Lords and their aides from far-off castles that had stayed another night rather than travel home in the dark. Baron Darcy swept into the room, with Lord Smallweed and Pogo behind him. They took their seats.

"Last night we reached an impasse," Darcy said. "I wonder whether having slept on it, we have any further ideas. I will go round the table and ask everyone to contribute an idea, however stupid it might seem to you. We will not judge these ideas, just write them on this board so we can all look at them. Maybe ideas will connect with each other and then we can build a solution together."

Everyone nodded and there was a general murmur too as they commented to their neighbour or just to the assembled group. "I've heard of this," muttered George to Fred. "It's called brainstorming." They both sat up, alert and interested.

"Let's start on my left and work round the table. Lady Nimrod?"

"We have to persuade Hugo to use a different export route," she said, and Pogo wrote this on the board.

"We could make our own drink to replace Wozna Cola," said Prince Lupin, and so it went round the table, with some people saying nothing and others making wild suggestions.

"We persuade Hugo (or Mariusz as I think that's his real name) to export Wozna to us in 2021, and we go without it till then." said George. Somebody laughed at him, but Pogo wrote up the idea just as he said it.

"We export Vex to Hattan and the West in 2021 and bring back Wozna on the return leg," said Fred. Stunned silence. After a few seconds, three of the Vexstein household stood up, bowed to Baron Darcy and left the room.

Baden passed his turn to make a suggestion and it was Pogo's turn.

"I have no further comment to make, save that my idea was nearly the same as these," he said, tapping the comments he had written up from Fred and George.

Lord Smallweed took the floor. "It is usual to discuss the merits of all the suggestions, but these two seem to have the merit of simplicity and economic justification. It would give Hugo (or Mariusz)," he added, nodding in George's direction, "a continuous profit line, and it would give Vex time to set up the necessary delivery chains, including cold storage vessels for transoceanic crossings. What do you say,

Prince Lupin?"

"I like the idea," said Lupin, "but we need to discover the effect on the population if Wozna were to be withdrawn from sale. Obviously, people like it. Yet if we substitute our own drink then it would change the market for Wozna in 2021 - which is after all twelve years away."

Lady Nimrod rose. "It is a hard choice, but currently people are suffering privation because of the Energy Drain. That is the priority. We must close this time tunnel and that means we must stop the trade in Wozna, or at least in Diet Wozna. If it means that to achieve this we go without a drink which a minority of citizens enjoy, then that is what must be done." She retook her seat to a muttering that appeared to be general agreement.

George shifted in his seat. He knew something that the others didn't, and he felt he had to keep it to himself. He knew that someone in the East would discover the power of strawberry juice very shortly. Other drinks would be needed as strawberry juice became more valuable. By 2021, the East might be crying out for a new drink such as Wozna. He wondered who would be the inventor of strawberry juice power.

Baron Darcy started speaking again, but stopped as two of the three that had left earlier re-entered the room. "What is it?" he asked.

"My lord, we desired to peruse the strategic plan for Vex Breweries and to see whether export to the West was a practical approach, or indeed whether it could be part of a vision for the 2020s," said one.

"We are pleased to say that following our latest trade mission earlier this year this remained an aspirational approach, although we had not set any targets at this stage," said the other.

"There are various technological developments needed," said the first.

"But we are confident these can be achieved," followed the second.

George relaxed. It looked like they were going to go along with this idea. They would probably invent strawberry juice power, as well. He felt a little sad that he would not have the honour, but it got him out of the difficulty of 'discovering' something from the future.

"Good," Baron Darcy said. "In that case, lady and gentlemen, I think we can close this meeting. Prince Lupin and his party will stay for lunch where we can discuss the strategy needed to persuade Hugo that this is the right course and that it is in his best interests to make this alliance with us. Thank you to the rest of you for joining us this morning. I hope you have pleasant journeys and arrive not too much later than you had originally intended." So saying he stood up, and walked towards the door. Everyone followed him. "Wait in the pink salon, if you don't mind," he said to Lady Nimrod and Prince Lupin, and Fred, George and Baden followed as Pogo showed them the way.

* * *

Saku took Victor and Argon up to the sky courtyard and then down to Mariusz's quarters.

"Let's see if we can persuade him to the right course," Saku said. He told them to wait at the door, and he knocked and went inside. After a few moments, he came back and waved them in. They crossed the room and Victor saw the person he knew as Hugo.

"This is my son Argon, and his son Victor, sire." Mariusz froze at the introductions, then got up from his sofa and walked over to them.

"*You* are the meddling barkeeper who I used to trust before I had to throw you into a dungeon last year," he said, pointing at Argon's chest. "And *you* are the bright spark I've seen grow from a stripling who I always thought was too clever to become a barkeeper," he said, pointing at Victor. "And you're all related!" he sat down again and waved them to some cushions. "So what do you want?"

"We would like to persuade you of the wisdom of not using the time tunnel to export Wozna to us, but to use land and sea routes to export in the same timeline," said Victor.

"And what of the time tunnel?"

"Well, it's a bit dangerous, isn't it?" said Saku. "We could do without the drain on our resources, and we always worried about it being unstable. If we only make enough Diet Wozna for Hattanites, then we shouldn't produce that much of a problem and the tunnel should close of its own accord. We could live within our means."

Mariusz sighed.

"I have been thinking about that ever since I got back and scared George off. I realised that time does its own thing, and we can't manipulate it. What's done is already done and it would be very dangerous to try and change that."

They all nodded in agreement. Mariusz seemed to be in a very thoughtful, accepting mood.

"I've been looking at the records around the year 2009, which I think is the year you come from, isn't that right Victor?"

Victor nodded.

"It seems that we had a formal trade visit a little earlier, from some people from a brewery in the East suggesting a mutual trade route; they imported Wozna for us, and we imported their new ale for them. We couldn't agree terms because the shipping arrangements were too costly and didn't have the right cooling processes. I guess the situation is the same now as then."

"Not necessarily, Hugo, I mean, sorry, Lord Mariusz," stammered Victor. "We could go back and persuade Vex Breweries of the value of developing the appropriate equipment to set up import-export routes for 2021."

Mariusz smiled. "That we could," he said, "but you will have to wait years for your next deliveries."

Victor looked gloomy. How could he persuade Vex Breweries to go along with this? "I think you need to come back one last time to persuade them, Hugo, I mean sir."

"Yeah, I think I do," Mariusz said, getting to his feet. "And what are you going to do, Argon? You've made yourself uncommon useful since I let you out. You'd be welcome to stay."

"I'm honoured at your invitation, sire," Argon said, "but I have an Inn to run, and it sounds like my boy has other paths to tread than that of a simple barkeeper."

"And you, Saku?" Mariusz asked.

"Oh yes, Saku, please come back with us, we could be a real family!" said Victor, practically bouncing up and down.

Saku smiled sadly. "I belong to this time, Victor, it would be wrong of me to return. I have already lived in 2009." He sighed and looked at Argon. "I am sorry I missed your growing up, your life, and I always missed you and your mother terribly. But the decision was made long ago, and it was made with the best intentions, whatever the outcome. I must not go back now. I am so glad to know you are well and happy though."

"How are you at running, you two? It would be good to be back at your inn by early evening, which I could do if we left now, but I don't know that you could keep up," Mariusz said.

"I have brought Dad's velocipede to the time tunnel, as I felt I needed to be back even sooner than that," said Victor. "What about you, Dad?"

"I could follow on at my own pace if Hugo's is too fast," Argon replied. "I'll get to the inn, I know the way."

So saying all four left Mariusz's quarters and went up to the time tunnel. It was a lovely morning on a late spring day in Hattan. Saku looked at them sadly. "I'm glad we will solve this problem of the Energy Drain," he said, "but it would have been nice to have been able to visit every now and then." He hugged Argon and Victor, pushing a piece of paper into Victor's hand. "Give this to George," he said. "Lord Mariusz is not the only one who has been looking in the records."

Victor nodded, and the three of them stepped towards the time tunnel.

Chapter 14: Return to the Inn

Dimerie 1999

In which Fred and George have to make a decision and Hugo reveals his true self

The carriage was rolling through open countryside having left the plains below Castle Vexstein. George, Fred and Baden were the advance party to warn the inn of their coming. They would send the carriage back for the Prince and Lady Nimrod and their attendants. Prince Lupin and Lord Smallweed were discussing the detailed plans with the Vex Breweries team on how they would develop the export arrangements, provided Lupin succeeded in getting Hugo to agree to their plan. They had agreed that tackling this tricky subject would need an excursion through the time tunnel, so the Inn was to become the centre of operations.

The conversation in the carriage moved on from the events of the day, and Baden asked George more about his trip to Hattan. He described the city and his trip to the diner (leaving out the incident on the way home), and the wondrous machines and methods for getting up and down the towers, but he steered clear of the subject of Wozna production, and in particular of the strawberry juice question. His main concern now was the 'when' of their trip to Hattan. "You see, Baden," he said, "as far as I can work out, if I go back, I will arrive very soon after I left. Lord Mariusz (or Hugo) will be trying to arrest me and throw me in the dungeon. If you guys come through at exactly the same time as me it will probably help to stop that happening, but Mariusz will still be angry, possibly more so because he missed me!" Baden agreed with him and George continued. "So it would probably be best if I didn't go back."

"When will we arrive if you don't come with us? Still just after you left?" he asked.

"I'm not sure," said George. "I think it works differently if you start from this side than if you start from Hattan," and he outlined his theories of the time tunnel.

Fred thought on this for a while as the carriage dropped down between steep sandy banks to enter the tunnel on the last stretch of the journey to the inn.

"I think you are close, but not in the gold," he said, referring to a target practice game they played in which the highest score was right in the middle, in the gold circle. "I think it hinges on Hugo's behaviour on the night we stayed at the inn. Instead of your theory, I think he had to run back, knowing you were on your way, to use your skills to fix the machine. He arrived before you because he had gone back to just after whenever he left in the first place. Then you arrived, but he had to come back here at a certain time in order to be back for breakfast, which is why Prince Lupin saw him emerging from the tunnel. So that's why he was so anxious to leave at midnight, to get back to the inn in time to go to Buckmore. No wonder he'd forgotten about me!" he chuckled, thinking of the amount of time Hugo had been on the go, and the enormous strain it must have placed him under.

"So if we go and visit," he continued, "I think we may arrive the same amount of time after Hugo (or you) left Castle Hattan as has gone by since you arrived back here. So two or is it three days will have gone by."

Baden had been following this and trying to count things on the fingers of either hand. He gave up. "I think you have a good point there, Fred, and you guys are cleverer than me anyway. We could use you at Castle Buckmore. Will you come and stay after this is sorted out?"

Fred and George looked at each other. Neither had given any thought to what would happen after their adventure. As most people do, if they had thought of it at all, they had assumed they would go back home and things would carry on as before.

Baden continued. "I see you haven't thought that far ahead. Well, I think it would be fun, and I'll talk to

Prince Lupin about it if you like. In any case, come and visit for a few days, weeks if you like. You deserve a holiday after all this dashing about."

The carriage pulled into the market square and Baden saw to the horses and the returning of the carriage to Vexstein whilst George and Fred went into the inn.

"Is Victor about?" they asked the worried looking person behind the bar.

"Um, no, not yet, but he's expected back, fingers crossed, begging your pardon." He sounded worried as well.

"But he got back from Castle Vexstein all right, didn't he?" asked George.

"Oh yes," said the barkeeper. "That was yesterday. But he went off on a mission late last night." He looked at them closely. "You are Fred and George from Castle Marsh, aren't you?" he asked and they nodded. "Well, I can give you this, then."

He opened the till and pulled out a message in Victor's handwriting as Baden came up and joined them. He ordered a couple of Vexes and a plate of crudités for them, then stayed behind to talk to the barkeeper as the Princelings took their drinks and food plus the note to a quiet table overlooking the square.

"Dear Prince Lupin, or whoever reads this note," they read. "I have decided to set off to the time tunnel to rescue my father, who was last seen going in that direction with Hugo. I think I will arrive on the second evening after George left Hattan. I am taking my velocipede down to the tunnel to get there and back as quickly as possible. If all goes well I should be back before the evening rush. If not, I'm sure Gandy will look after things until I return. With most humble respects, Victor Barton" and scribbled at the bottom there was a P.S. "I think Hugo and Mariusz are the same person."

They looked at each other, and then handed the note to Baden as he sat down after arranging with Gandy for Prince Lupin and Lady Nimrod's comfort for the night, plus their own.

Baden whistled as he finished it. "Wow, he's got courage that lad. How does the time fit with your theory?"

"I agree with him entirely," said Fred, who had been working it out in his head. "But it suggests that if we went down the tunnel after him at say, 11 tonight, even using the carriage we would be at least a day behind him."

"Well, Prince Lupin and Lady Nimrod should be here around 6 this evening," said Baden. "It's possible that Victor might arrive back around then if he got his timing right and his mission went well. Let's hope it did."

They settled back and enjoyed their snack, having left before lunch was served at Vexstein. They talked once more about the possibility of persuading Hugo to what they now referred to as the Vexstein trade plan, and couldn't see what he would have against it, unless time travel had become something he valued in itself. George described the souvenirs in his apartment.

"Well, we can always find him some gifts to add to the collection," Baden had added. "And he can travel on the vessel if he chooses."

"Not quite as quick or convenient." said George.

"But having all that time here and then going back to a moment later at Hattan must be terribly tiring, and wearing on the body too," suggested Fred.

They also talked about life at Buckmore, how Baden passed his time, and what they would do if they went to Buckmore for an extended period. It sounded interesting, and they would be more in the way of things going on, meet more travellers and so on, than they ever would at the Castle in the Marsh.

"I think we might find it a little boring just looking at the reeds after all this," said Fred, wistfully.

"And I can't see Uncle Vlad accepting we'd had any part in solving the Energy Drain, so we'd be back to skulking and hiding," added George. "Maybe we could come, at least for a short while, and then go travelling if we outstayed our welcome."

"Doesn't Castle Marsh get any news from the rest of the world?" Baden asked. "Surely it'll be in the papers that you were instrumental in solving the problem, once Prince Lupin and the Barons tell everyone."

George and Fred exchanged glances once more.

"What are papers?" Fred asked.

The rest of the afternoon was spent in acquiring a copy of the various newspapers stocked in the market, and poring over them, comparing styles and approaches, regional versus national coverage, and content generally. A couple had pages devoted to science and technology. These were new words to Fred and George but they found they fitted perfectly with their understanding of natural philosophy and engineering, so they went back to see if there were any other editions of those papers they could read. Baden had gone to check the facilities for the Buckmore arrival, as Gandy was becoming overwhelmed with anxiety at the responsibility of not only being solely responsible for the inn but also having important guests, when Fred and George saw Victor suddenly come out of the tunnel on the most amazing two-wheeled contraption. George didn't know which he wanted to do first, find out how Victor had fared in Hattan, or examine the machine. He decided the machine could wait, and they followed Victor around until he had spoken to Gandy (to the latter's huge relief), checked the rooms for Prince Lupin and Lady Nimrod (and pronounced them perfect, to Gandy's even huger relief) and checked the tally of rooms left for the night, crossing another of the high status ones off the list.

"Who's that for?" said Fred.

"You'll see soon enough," replied Victor with a hint of smugness in his tone.

Just then the clock in the square struck six, a carriage arrived at the Inn from the Corey-Vexstein Line and a staging coach arrived from the Fortune-Dimerie Line, so that there was total chaos in the square. Victor and Gandy were so busy with the general

travellers that Baden settled Prince Lupin and Lady
Nimrod in their very nicely appointed rooms and
came down to tell Fred and George that they should
go up in five minutes.

"We need to hear what Victor has been up to as soon
as possible, if not sooner," Lupin said, looking up
from Victor's note. Fred had handed it to him after
he had briefed them all on the plans he had mapped
out with Vex Breweries that afternoon. Baden
nipped out to fetch Victor, and while they waited,
Prince Lupin asked the princelings what they would
do after their adventure.

"We hadn't really thought about it until Baden asked
in the carriage," Fred replied carefully. "We really
enjoy our work, philosophising and engineering, but
we discovered there are other people who do this and
exchange ideas in the papers, only they call it science
and technology."

Lupin smiled. "Yes, you do seem to have been rather
cut off from things in Castle Marsh. You could help
to bring them into the 21st century. But maybe you
need to explore a little first."

"We have been wondering," said Lady Nimrod,
"whether the old laboratories in our castle could be
refurbished to give you scope for new and exciting
discoveries. You would have a home in our castle,
and enjoy the same sort of status as Baden does. He
is also a refugee from an antiquated system."

Fred didn't need to look at George to know his
reaction to the words 'laboratories could be
refurbished.' A place he could really work on his

ideas was something George dreamed of. And Fred thought that philosophising from the ramparts of Castle Buckmore would be spectacular!

"You don't need to make a decision now," said Lupin. "In fact we need to see how this turns out. If Hugo, or Mariusz rather, won't play ball, we have a severe problem."

Just then, there was a knock on the door, and Victor put his head round. "Begging your pardon, Prince Lupin, but do you mind if we wait just a little longer for me to tell you what happened at Castle Hattan?"

"No, not at all," said Lupin, although you could see he was itching to find out. "Just send up a bottle or two of the Dimerie 1999, would you, please?" and Victor withdrew. Shortly afterwards Gandy brought up a tray with three bottles of the wine Lupin had asked for, plus eight glasses.

"Now what is Victor up to?" Lupin asked, counting the glasses. "He knows there are only five of us."

Baden had just finished passing round four glasses of wine, and had poured his own, when a knock came again at the door.

"Come in!" called Lupin.

Victor held the door open as Hugo, or Mariusz, walked in, and Victor said "May I present Lord Mariusz of Castle Hattan, Prince Lupin?"

Everyone stood up as Mariusz walked in and bowed to Prince Lupin. Victor followed him in grinning at the effect his little surprise had had.

"Urr, well, hi," said Mariusz somewhat bashfully, "I guess it's about time I came clean with you guys, and let you know of the plan that Victor has made with me."

Lupin waved him to a seat on his right, and they all sat down. Victor poured two more glasses of wine, and handed one to Mariusz.

"We have been thinking about how to keep your Wozna export line to the East open," Lupin began.

"So have I," Mariusz interjected, "and I need your help to persuade the Vex guys to play a part in it."

As Lupin looked at Mariusz, astounded, and Mariusz returned his gaze, somewhat hopefully, Lady Nimrod put the vital question: "If we can arrange a mutual export-import route between you and Vex for 2021, could you stop production of Diet Wozna right now?"

The answer, it seemed was yes, and although there were many more details to be gone into, assurances, drafting of contracts dated for the future, the main effect was to have everyone raising their glasses and talking happily about the agreement between Castle Hattan and Vex Breweries. The agreement was supported by both Vexstein and Buckmore (who seemed to have a business interest in Vexstein as well as a general desire to do good).

One glass stood empty on the table.

"Who is that last glass for, Victor," asked Nimrod.

"Um, my Dad, Argon, if you don't mind him joining us later, my lady," said Victor, coyly, and they all congratulated him on a successful mission. They broke into little groups for more chatting, with Victor joining Baden and the princelings. Victor outlined how he'd met both Argon and Saku, and they talked about families for a bit. Then Victor produced a piece of paper, which he handed to George.

"Saku asked me to give you this. He said he'd been looking in the records."

George unfolded a scrap of paper. It was a newspaper cutting, dated January 23rd 2011.

"Breakthrough in power production" ran the headline, and underneath a picture of George shaking hands with Prince Lupin: "Buckmore technologist George Marsh unveils revolutionary new power plant running on strawberry juice."

He folded it carefully and put it away, even though Fred looked hurt that he hadn't passed it round. He'd show him privately later. The great benefit of time travel, he thought, feeling immensely relaxed and at peace with the world, was that some decisions were much easier when you knew that, sometime in the future, you had already made them.

Chapter 15: Epilogue

Lord Mariusz's
Salon

In which Mariusz receives some visitors

Mariusz sipped some Wozna Cola in the sweltering heat of a July in Hattan. He discovered he actually preferred it to Diet, which they had discontinued some eight weeks earlier. They hadn't made any big fuss about it in the press, and no one had really noticed it in the city. Saku was working on a new recipe that he said never put the calories in, so there would be none to take out.

The time tunnel had disappeared. Well, the gateway was still there, but the ring of little lights had gone. Someone had found it was a good place to store drinks for the courtyard when there was a reception or some other function, as it was generally nice and cool in there.

He stood up and moved to a window where he gazed onto the scurrying masses of Hattan Island far below. The glare from the rivers made him glad of the filmy gauze material he'd imported from that Indian Rajah who liked Wozna so much he'd negotiated his first franchise deal with him.

His young nephew, Raisin, interrupted his thoughts.

"There's some people to see you, Uncle Mariusz. On business, they said."

"Show them in then, Raisin." Mariusz settled himself on his sofa and nodded to an assistant who went off to prepare refreshments for all.

Raisin returned, followed by two people.

"Uncle Mariusz, may I present Baron Pogo of Vexstein, and Victor Barton, the Export Manager of Vex Breweries?"

Mariusz smiled as he welcomed the visitors.

"Urr, well, hi," he said. "I've been kinda expecting you."

THE END

Look out for the next part of the Princelings trilogy:
The Princelings and the Pirates

and the final part of the trilogy is:
The Princelings and the Lost City

The series continues, with more adventures in the Realms, and more mysteries for Fred, George and their friends to unravel.
The Traveler in Black and White
The Talent Seekers
Bravo Victor

Read more about and by Jemima Pett and get background to the Princelings' world on her blog
http://jemimapett.com
Follow on Twitter @jemima_pett

The Princelings official website is at
http://princelings.co.uk

Follow the Princelings stories on Facebook
http://www.facebook.com/Princelings

Did you enjoy this book? Why not leave a review at your favourite reading site?

Read the start of *The Princelings and the Pirates* by Jemima Pett

In which we meet Princess Kira and she meets disaster with equanimity

"There's a noise of oars or something, I tell you!" Princess Kira turned away from the window where she'd been peering out into the mist. "I'm sure something's going on out there."

"But nobody's sounded an alarm, Kira. You've just got the jitters because it looks spooky out tonight."

Kira crossed the room and jumped into bed next to her sister, Princess Nerys.

"Oh, maybe," she said, shrugging her shoulders and looking at the window again. "You can't see a thing out there though. It would be a great night for them to attack."

"And just who is 'them'?" asked Nerys in a scolding tone. "You know Miles and Morris said there were no such things as pirates and the people on the shore were just being hysterical."

"Well, I don't know, but what they were saying about the wine being stolen and the vineyards being overrun sounded pretty much like raiders from the sea to me, and if that's not pirates, what are they?"

Nerys said nothing. Her sister had a good point there. Things had been bad for the past few weeks and her father, King Helier, her brothers and all the courtiers had been deep in discussions from which, on the whole, the two eldest princesses had been excluded. They'd been frustrated at not knowing the details. Usually their brothers kept them informed so they'd be well-trained when they eventually had castles to run themselves. For their husbands, of course.

Kira got out of bed again and returned to the window. Before she could get there it broke into hundreds of pieces and a leg appeared through it, followed by a body. More legs and bodies followed. The room seemed filled with large, smelly strangers with long smelly hair. Some of them had swords.

Get The Princelings and the Pirates to read more!

Read the start of *The Princelings and the Lost City* by Jemima Pett

Fred gazed out of the window along the road to Powell. It wasn't his normal window and it wasn't his normal gaze: instead of Thinking, he was Watching, and watching impatiently too. Beside him, also watching, but in a state of contained excitement, was his brother George.

Princess Kira was arriving shortly. She had told them that her brother would be driving a new type of carriage, and that they would arrive on the straight stretch of road approaching the castle, and would they please warn everyone that they might need to stand aside if the carriage wasn't completely under control. Fred hadn't the faintest idea what she meant by that, and was frantic for her safety.

Get The Princelings and the Lost City to read more!

Author Jemima Pett

I've been writing stories, creating articles and event reports for newsletters and magazines ever since I was eight years, but early fiction attempts failed for want of suitable inspiration: I just couldn't find interesting characters and plot! I had a series of careers in business that kept me chained to a desk for many years. I wrote manuals, reports, science papers, blogs, journals, anything and everything that kept the words flowing. Finally, the characters jumped into my head with stories that needed to be told, and THE PRINCELINGS OF THE EAST was born.

I now live in Norfolk, England, with my six guinea pigs, successors to the originals, Fred, George, Hugo (pictured) and Victor.

I am currently working on Book 7, provisionally called The Chronicles of Willoughby the Narrator.